HE SODBURY CRUCIFIX

agricultural depths of Gloucestershire, one town and four villages called ıry are located, mysterious happenings A peculiar little metal cross is found by ıyside, and revolutionary events affect es of everyone whose hands it comes For example, the well-known atheist, ı Colquhoun, discusses the cross dir̃ vectfully at his peril, and poor Ruby Sim̤ ıns believes her possession of the cross ha̤ ̧ ven her a second chance. The question is wl. ther all the changes for the better or the worse are mere coincidences, or manifestations of the supernatural.

THE SODBURY CRUCIFIX

THE SODBURY CRUCIFIX

by

Julian Fane

Dales Large Print Books
Long Preston, North Yorkshire,
BD23 4ND, England.

British Library Cataloguing in Publication Data.

Fane, Julian
    The Sodbury crucifix.

A catalogue record of this book is
available from the British Library

ISBN   1-84262-357-5 pbk

First published in Great Britain 2004 by The Book Guild Ltd.

Copyright © Julian Fane 2004

Cover illustration © Anthony Monaghan

The right of Julian Fane to be identified as the author of this
work has been asserted by him in accordance with the
Copyright, Designs and Patents Act, 1988

Published in Large Print 2005 by arrangement with
The Book Guild Ltd.

Dales Large Print is an imprint of Library Magna Books Ltd.

Printed and bound in Great Britain by
T.J. (International) Ltd., Cornwall, PL28 8RW

To
Thetis Blacker
with particular thanks for elucidating some
of the mysteries of the number 7

Contents

The Pot

This story is stranger than fiction.

It began not long ago, in the month of January, and had run its course within the same year.

The scene of the action was a small area of South Gloucestershire in the West of England. Everything happened within approximately five or six square miles, marked out by one town, the ancient market town of Chipping Sodbury, three villages, Old Sodbury, Little Sodbury and Lower Sodbury, and one hamlet, Sodbury on the Hill. Three of the Sodburys are located in the Vale: Chipping, Old and Lower – the Vale being the extensive flat plain that reaches to the southern bank of the mouth of the River Severn. Little Sodbury clings to the sharply rising ground at the eastern limit of the Vale, and Sodbury on the Hill stands on the plateau above.

The name Sodbury refers not to the agricultural sod and has no connection with the Cities of the Plain in the Bible, although comedians have mocked it for both reasons. Historians suggest that it describes the 'burg', that is the borough or the lands, of

'Soppa', who seems to have been either a person or a place. Historically, otherwise, the Gloucestershire Sodburys are unremarkable. They used to be, and to a certain extent remain, larger and smaller agricultural communities, despite Chipping Sodbury's stone quarries and the lure of the industries of Yate and Bristol.

It was therefore hardly surprising that the overture to the drama or melodrama or phenomenon or whatever it was should be set in train on a farm. The farmer was called Iles. He rented some five hundred acres from the Badminton Estate, and lived in the pleasant house attached to the farmyard situated half a mile or so from Sodbury on the Hill.

Sam Iles, who tilled the land of so-called Sodbury Holding, was an authoritative brawny middle-aged man, grizzled, red-faced, jovial and shrewd – he looked as if he had been type-cast to play the role of a rustic John Bull. Sam, a widower for the past decade, lived with his housekeeper, Nelly Palmer. He had advertised for a housekeeper in *The Farmer and Stockbreeder*, tried out two applicants for the job, who were not willing to sleep with their potential boss, then struck lucky with Nell. She was the widow of a farmer, was used to country ways, and she and Sam had been comfortable together for three years. They worked hours that would have horrified a Trade Unionist – and he sometimes acknowledged that she was busier than he was, keeping house, shopping, acting as milkmaid, hen wife, and occasional shepherdess. Sam was fifty-five, Nelly fifty. Sam's son and only child, Tom, had gone to study American farming methods in Texas.

Sam Iles, with help from Nell and his one employee, Dan Green, ran the farm. They ploughed and sowed, made hay and harvested, milked the herd of Friesian cows, attended to a flock of sheep, a few pigs and the poultry. He was old-fashioned, he followed in the footsteps of his father, the previous tenant of Sodbury Holding, and called in professionals to cut his corn and carry animals to market.

The single employee, Dan Green, was as typical as his employer. He was the red-cheeked heavily-built farm boy of inter-national art and the popular imagination. He was also honest, forthright, uncomplaining and good-humoured, and had recently married a girl almost as strong as he was, Peggy, who worked for Wilkin Smith, the timber merchant in Yate. Dan was twenty-five and Peggy twenty-two. They had been sweethearts long before they tied the knot, but she had succeeded in retaining her virginity until she could see the ring on her finger.

The Greens lived, and were getting to know each other, in the tied bungalow behind the milking shed. The decision taken by Dan's predecessor, Will Stamp, to retire and vacate the bungalow, and Mr Iles's offer to let Dan have it when he was married, counted for more with the young couple than their romantic yearnings. Realism inspired Dan to pop the question and liberate himself from life with his parents, and Peggy to become a missis and have a home of her own.

Matrimony suited them quite nicely – they were not prone to torture themselves with regrets. He was nice to her as long as she prepared his sandwiches in the morning and had his tea ready for him at six o'clock, and she was glad to get her hands on his wages. Watching TV together in the evenings was easy, and she was growing less averse to paying the price for her new and satisfying status.

The weather was murky on a particular Monday morning. It had been damp for weeks when it was not raining, and a nagging little wind from the east seemed to be understudying the sun. Dan drove the tractor to the far corner of the Big Field, dismounted and plodded round the overgrown greenery, almost a thicket, that encircled the pond called Hetty's Pot. The pond, the Pot, was about ten metres across, fringed with rushes and willow trees, not deep, and always full of clear spring water, any excess of which trickled into a dyke sprouting vegetation. The Pot was well-known locally, and frequented by lovers in summer and sometimes by picnic parties for children. Agriculturally, it was an extremely useful amenity for Sodbury Holding – its tenant farmers had immemorially put their cattle out to graze in the Big Field and to drink Pot water.

Beyond it, on land that did not belong to Sam Iles' farm, was a cart track or bridleway reaching from Sodbury on the Hill to the park of Badminton House.

Dan's job was to trim back trees and bushes, so that the Iles cows could reach the water and the cart track should not be blocked by verdure. He walked round the part of the Pot within the Big Field, judging the amount of cutting he would have to do, then climbed over a strand of sagging barbed wire. Dawn had begun to break, and a robin was sufficiently wide awake to float its song on the silence. Dan was used to birds singing, he took no notice of the robin, but heard another sound, a worrying growl or whimper, unrecognisable for a second or two. He stood in the cart track and listened. He strained his ears and heard somebody cry, 'Help!'

17

A dry stone wall ran along the other side of the track on land belonging to another farmer, Mr Steve Judson.

Dan Green, having looked to his right and left and spotted no clue to the cry for help, now noticed a few Cotswold stones missing and dislodged on top of the wall, and at the same time heard another groan trailing off into a whimper. He crossed the track and peered over the wall, saw a booted leg, hoisted himself up to get a better view and looked down on a man lying on his front on the grass, his bloody face twisted to one side and the booted leg at such an unnatural angle to the body that it sickened him.

'Oh my,' he exclaimed, 'what you been and done?'

He clambered into the meadow and saw a motorbike on its side and skid marks in the grass.

The man was a youth, his black hair muddy, wearing leather motoring gear, bomber jacket and knee-high boots with fancy silver fastenings.

'Cold,' he mumbled.

'How long you been out here?'

'Last night...'

'Oh my,' Dan repeated, removing his grubby anorak and spreading it on the back of the youth. As he did so he said: 'You were lucky Mr Judson didn't turn his bullocks out in the field. I'll go and tell where you are fast as I can.'

'My leg...'

'You've broke it – so you stay put till they come and get you,' Dan said.

'Tell me another,' the youth whispered, but with a trace of spirit.

Dan returned to the tractor and drove back to Sodbury Holding. He found Sam and Nelly in the milking shed, washing up after the cows had been milked, and told his tale. Sam went to ring for an ambulance, Nelly to make hot sweet tea, then lent Dan a coat, and they all three climbed into the tractor and headed for Hetty's Pot.

Needless to say the youth had obeyed Dan's instruction, he had not moved, he could not move. His condition was shocking – apart from his broken leg, he had a deep cut in the middle of his forehead, his left arm appeared to be out of commission, and he had had to yield to one of the calls of nature where he lay. He rejected Sam's offer to try to turn him face upwards, he squawked at the thought, and was unable to swallow much of Nelly's tea offered in the cap of the thermos.

While they waited for an ambulance, which would have to come from Chipping Sodbury and reach the scene of the accident as best it could, Dan collected his billhook from the tractor and set to work on trimming the brambles and branches obstructive of a vehicle's progress up the track, Sam rang Steve Judson on his mobile, and Nell jumped to conclusions.

Farmer Judson's contribution to the crisis was negative. He arrived in his usual grumpy mood, complained of the skidding, insisted on having the motorbike thrown off his field and over his wall, bent down to examine the face of the injured youth and pronounced that he could be Matt Conley, a rogue and burglar notorious in the Tetbury area.

His parting shot to the Ileses was to shout over his shoulder: 'They better look lively to cart him away, because I'll be pasturing my Toby hereabouts in next to no time' – Toby was the name of his prize bull.

Nell's more feminine and fanciful conclusions were that the motorbike must have flown over the wall, for she could find no signs of how it had landed where it did. And, considering the speed at which it must have been travelling, the rider surely would have fallen farther into the field. Her third conclusion simply reinforced Farmer Judson's opinion, for the left-hand pocket of the youth's leather trousers had been torn open and a pile of money had spilled out, small change and a few fivers. The prostrate figure also had loot in his right-hand trouser pocket. The probability was that Matt, after stealing someone's savings, had been taking a secretive route homewards when he crashed.

Nelly asked him about the money, and he replied: 'That's mine.'

'It's on the ground,' she said.

'I know,' he whined, 'but I can't use that hand.'

'Shall I pick it up?'

'Yeah, but its mine.'

'I know – and I'm more honest than I think you are.'

The ambulance men arrived eventually and on foot. Their lift of Matt on to the stretcher, the essential preparations beforehand, the negotiation of the wall, and the inevitably bumpy trip down the track, were painful in the extreme. Matt squealed and hollered all the way.

One result of the excitement on that Monday morning was that Dan Green did not complete the task of cutting back the greenery round Hetty's Pot. A second one, a consequence of the first, was that as cattle could not easily get at the water in the Pot the herd was not allowed into the adjacent part of the Big Field. But before long Sam Iles wanted to put his cows there, and one afternoon he drove Dan in the tractor to inspect the Pot and decide exactly how many branches and how much undergrowth had to be removed.

It was a nice enough day, sunny but crisp – the weather had been nice ever since the accident. The two men inspected the pseudo-oasis from the outside, then forced their way through briar roses, brambles and whippy twigs.

The pond was half empty. They were astonished and dismayed. They expressed their feelings Gloucestershire fashion.

Sam asked rhetorically: 'What's up here?' And Dan remarked: 'That's a funny thing.'

Then they became more conversational than usual.

Sam said: 'Never happened before in my time, no more in my father's.'

Dan reminded him: 'It was wet in December, too – there's been water to keep it filled.'

'Could be the spring's going dry,' Sam suggested, and Dan echoed: 'Could be.'

But they were not country people for nothing, they were soon suspicious, they suspected they were the victims of foul play.

'Who's been at it?' Sam wanted to know, and answered his own question: 'That Judson, he's been digging out his ditches, he'd like nothing better than to stick his dirty finger in our pie, sure as eggs he blames us for the motorbike in his field and the stone off his wall.'

'I'd like to catch the blighter that done it,' Dan said.

'Might be boys from the village,' Sam allowed. 'I'd give them a walloping – if the Pot's finished I'll be paying a fortune to pipe water across the Big Field.'

'Where do springs come from, Mr Iles?' Dan inquired.

'They come from deep down – but you and me now, we better look where our water's gone.'

They circled the pond with difficulty and inspected the drain leading towards the dyke that had absorbed the overflow in the good old days. Clearly no water had passed through it recently – the earth was so dry as to have cracked in places. And they found not a trace of intrusion by foreign bodies, no footprints or breakages or vandalism or litter. The whole place, pond and surrounding thicket, and even the cart track on its far side, was as undisturbed and peaceful as ever; and the silence began to seem queer.

Sam and Dan shook their heads and drove back to the Holding, where their womenfolk linked the water or lack of it with the accident.

Nelly Palmer was still irked by the mystery of the flying motorbike, and she blamed witchcraft. There were witches in Sodbury on the Hill, she was in no doubt about that, and for reasons of their own they had put a curse on a piece of land not to their liking. Maybe she was being illogical, maybe she was not making sense – but, she insisted, witches would not be witches if they were sensible. She strongly advised Sam to have the Pot exorcised without delay and before it brought him to ruination.

Dan Green's wife Peggy over-reacted to Nell's over-reaction. Additionally, she was told by someone at work that long ago Hetty herself had been charged with being a witch and thrown into the Pot to prove her innocence or guilt – she sank because she was innocent and drowned. Such stories worked her into a 'doodah', and she began to complain of a loss of appetite for food, unique in her experience. She expressed fear that a spell had been cast upon Dan for mixing with ghosts, and when he emitted amorous signals she shouted at him, 'Nothing doing!'

A weekend came round. Peggy helped Nell with housework for a couple of hours on Saturday mornings. On the Saturday morning in question she was sick after breakfast, and convinced she was going to die.

'You've killed me, you and your Pot, you have, Dan, and I'll never let you off for it wherever I be.'

At nine she stumbled across to the farmhouse and regaled Nell with the symptoms that she believed were the harbingers of death.

Nell laughed and said she was probably pregnant, whereupon both women cheered up and drank cups of comforting coffee with fresh cream from the cows.

It was early days for Peggy, according to Dr Wood in Chipping Sodbury. She continued to work, but her nerves were on edge, now for two reasons instead of one. The baby was coming along too soon, before she and Dan were ready or could easily afford it.

Farmwork preoccupied Sam Iles for a week or so, but on a fine winter's afternoon he said he could spare Dan to go along to check the Pot.

Dan drove the tractor, parked it as usual, and struggled through the undergrowth. The pond was empty, and the mud on the bottom had formed a crust. Here and there white branches, stripped of their bark and looking like bones, were stuck in it, and bottles and a tin or two were also visible. He could not find the original source of the water, nothing was understandable, he recalled the talk of witches, began to feel uneasy, was aware of pricking at the back of his neck, and turned to leave in a hurry.

As he was doing so, a beam of the low sun shone through the leafless trees and was reflected into his eyes by an object in the centre of the muddy depression. He spotted it, a shiny spiky little thing, and without further consideration, almost involuntarily, as he tried to explain later on, he walked right into the pond or rather the mud pie – luckily he wore wellies. The thing was a metal cross. When he had rubbed off the mud, he saw coloured inserts, six of them, one missing. He heaved himself through the mud under the crust and reached what had been dry land. The cross fitted into the palm of his large hand, and had two sort of marbles and one hole in the vertical bar, and a couple of smaller marbles in the horizontal on the right and another couple on the left. He slipped it into his pocket and walked home, to the farm bungalow where he lived, not to the farmhouse.

Peggy was there – she had not felt well in the morning and had taken the day off. She was going to ask about the water when he produced the cross and handed it to her.

'Ooh!' she exclaimed.

'Like it?' he asked.

'Ask a silly question! Beautiful, Dan! Where d'you get it?'

He told her.

'It's finders keepers,' she said at once.

He took a different line. 'I'll have to show Sam, it's his by rights.'

She thrust it into the capacious bra she was wearing and said: 'I'm not giving it up.'

Dan thought better of fighting his wife to regain possession of the trinket, went to look for Sam and found him with Nell in the milking shed.

'I've been along to the Pot,' he said.

'Oh ar?' Sam queried in Gloucestershire lingo.

'Water's all gone.'

'What's that?'

'Water's gone.'

'Never!'

'I'm telling you.'

'Well – beats me.'

'I picked up something funny there.'

'Did you?'

'Jewellery.'

'Jewellery?'

'A cross.'

'Let's see it, Dan.'

'Peg's got it. It's round in the bungalow.'

'We better see it. We'll see it right away, before anyone gets the wrong idea.'

When the four of them were all together in the bungalow's lounge, Sam overcame Peggy's reluctance to show the item by means of the following speech.

'Listen here, the law is that anything of value found on the farm belong to the land-owner. I'm not touching what's the property of the Badminton Estate, and getting my fingers burnt. Peggy, you remember! If there's no value, it's a different matter.'

The cross was produced and exhibited. The six beads set into the metal were of different sizes, the two in the vertical were larger and the one in the middle was purple and the bottom one green, and the four in the horizontal were smaller and rose-coloured, yellow, blue and darker red.

Everyone admired it. Nell, who had a crush on the Duke of Beaufort, said she would be more than willing to present it to His Grace at Badminton House. But Peggy objected violently, and yelled in her loud voice, 'Over my dead body!' Sam called for peace, and ruled that the cross must have been tossed into the pond because it had a bead missing, that it had laid in the water for God knew how long because it was obviously worthless, and therefore Peggy was entitled not to hand it over.

The matter was settled, except for the waterlessness of the Pot.

Time passed. Three weeks later Peggy was suitably broody, but the broodier she became the more she worried. She had been buying the equipment of motherhood, and was frightened by the expense. She was really scared to have run up an overdraft at the bank, and she still had to buy a pram. She begged Dan in vain to put in for a rise in his wage. As her own employer had been kind about maternity leave and promised to give her back her job when she was again fit to do it, she was deterred from badgering him for money.

One Saturday morning Fred Croggett, the mechanic and dealer in cars and all saleable merchandise, drove up to Sodbury Holding to check Mr Iles' machinery before the spring.

He parked his truck in the farmyard just as Peggy was putting some washing on the line in the bungalow's front garden. He ambled across to talk to her. He was in his fifties, wore boots with metal toecaps, a blue overall and a grubby T-shirt, and had his customary small cigar clamped between his teeth. He had stubble on his chin and seemed to be soaked in sump oil, but his expression was confident, there was a naughty twinkle in his eye, his hair was brown and curly, and he was supposed to have sired a large percentage of the children of Sodbury on the Hill. He was also clever with cars, and he and Peggy had been acquainted ever since she could remember.

'Morning, Mr Croggett.'

'When you going to drop the Mister, Peggy?'

'I'm sure I don't know, Mr Croggett.'

'Well, we can see about that. All right, my love?'

'Yes, thanks. Yourself?'

'Still at it.'

'I'll have to get on, Mr Croggett.'

'Something to ask you, Peggy.' He removed the cigar and a wet trace of tobacco from his lips deliberately, and alarmed her with a searching look. 'What's this I hear about a jewel?'

'I don't know. What jewel? Who's been telling you stories?'

'Nelly Palmer tipped off my Glenys down the town.' Glenys was Fred's daughter. She was an unmarried mother who lived either with him in every sense, according to gossip, or had separate quarters in his premises along the Tetbury Road. The town referred to was Chipping Sodbury.

'She did, did she?' Peggy returned as discouragingly as she could. 'Did she indeed!'

'You still got it, Peggy?'

'I might have or I might not.'

'Not sold it yet?'

'There's no value to it, Mr Croggett.'

'I can tell you what it's worth – I done deals with women before now, they're my speciality.'

'Oh, you terrible man! I'm not saying any more to you.'

'Go on! I'm reading your face. You fetch it and I'll price it for no fee.'

'I'll put my washing out and see.'

'Take your time, my dear. I don't offer bargains too often, but I'll give you a minute or two.'

Peggy delayed for about half a minute, then went indoors and returned with the cross. She held it up and waved it this way

30

and that as if to tantalise.

'Pity it's not complete,' he said.

'I told you it has no value.'

'It's pretty enough, and old, too. Mind if I hold it?'

'You take care.'

'That I will. I always do, Peg – I'm a gentleman. Got a nice feel, hasn't it?'

'What are they, Mr Croggett, those stones, are they precious at all?'

'They're glass – you don't see much of precious stones that size. Tell the truth, you weren't far wrong – not a lot of value there.'

'You give it back, please.'

'I'd say fifty.'

'Eh?'

'Fifty pounds for it.'

'No!'

She disbelieved him – she had expected him to say five or something like it – but he must have thought she was haggling.

'I could make it a hundred to you,' he suggested with a wink.

'Oh, Mr Croggett, are you offering or what?'

'Question is, are you selling? Is it yours to sell? What about your Dan?'

'He's not having my baby, he's got no say.'

'Anyone else with a claim?'

'No!' She shut out thoughts of the Duke of Beaufort. 'No – I'd sell it if it was private and the price was right.'

'What for, dear?'

She took a deep breath.

'Hundred and fifty.'

'Done!'

She shook his hot and oily paw squeamishly. He produced a wad of notes and counted seven twenties and a ten with much licking of his thumb. She was flattered by being called a hard-headed woman, and by thinking she had got the better of Fred Croggett. She gloated over her hundred and fifty pounds, which cleared her overdraft and left her forty to spend on her baby's pram.

Fred Croggett was expected to return to Sodbury Holding a week after he bought the cross. The evening prior to his arrival sharpened the prickings of Peggy Green's conscience and her fears of being found out. The Croggetts were not a trustworthy breed, they might have spilled beans in every direction, and Dan could soon be in the know – he could even be told tomorrow.

She repeated to herself that their baby would get the benefit of the money, that she had the right to spend it, and Dan's involvement was over and done with. But he had been voicing peculiar ideas lately, that the cross was not just a jewel or a trinket, and that it might have the power to do them a favour or two. Therefore she was anxious, and increasingly so, to break the news to him herself, to defend her actions, and not to let him get hold of a garbled or malicious account and the wrong end of the stick.

She cooked a specially tasty tea for him, and made her confession in fairly aggressive terms. He was angry with her and, as inarticulate strong men do, he expressed his anger physically, by slapping her and resorting to fisticuffs when she slapped back.

The next day she miscarried.

At Fred's Dump

Peggy Green's miscarriage was not a discreet physiological episode and a private family grief.

It had been a stormy February night, meteorologically as well as in the Greens' bungalow. The wind got up and rain bucketed down. The weather was better, though still grey, in the morning, when Sam and Nell were milking the cows and Dan was letting out the poultry. Peggy's roar of pain and misery sounded bovine – Sam thought it was caused by a cow in distress; but Dan heard it and ran across the yard, shouting to Nell to follow him.

They administered first aid and sympathy. As soon as possible, Dan drove Peggy in their almost vintage Ford Fiesta to Tetbury Hospital. During that drive she made him swear never to tell anybody she had sold the cross, and they passed Fred Croggett in his pick-up truck heading for Sodbury Holding.

Fred tinkered with the farm machinery for four hours, then was invited by Sam into the farmhouse for cheese sandwiches and tea. They ate in the kitchen – Nell put newspaper on the seat of Fred's chair, she disapproved of his dirty habits and appearance, and had only agreed to provide dinner, as they called it, because Sam was keen to pick his brain.

They munched methodically and in silence to start with. Over cups of tea the conversation took a livelier turn.

'How's Glenys?' Nell inquired.

'All right,' Fred replied.

'How's her youngest? What's her name?'

'Rose.'

'How old would she be?'

'Six year old.'

'Glenys says you're fond of her.'

'She's all right.'

Sam spoke: 'Nice drop of rain last night.'

'Useful,' Fred agreed.

'Your business all right?'

'Ticking over. Yours?'

'Same here.'

Nelly put her oar in: 'Peggy Green lost her baby this morning.'

'Why's that?'

'You know her, don't you? I saw you talking to her last week.'

'I talk to all the females.'

'So you do, that's the trouble. Did Peggy have anything interesting to say?'

'Not to notice.'

'She didn't show you anything?'

'It was too early in the morning.'

'Fred Croggett, you're a disgrace!'

Sam intervened: 'You ever heard of Matt Conley?'

'I got his bike.'

'Our Dan was the one who found him in the field.'

'Steve Judson was on about that.'

'Steve Judson don't know the half of it. That's to say, I hope he don't know more than he should. Hetty's Pot mean much to you, Fred?'

'Can't say it does.'

'It's empty, no water there no more.'

'Something new, isn't it?'

'Never happened before. Like to have a look? I'll be thankful for your opinion.'

Sam supplied more information as he drove Fred across the Big Field in the tractor. He related that the Pot had drained away in two stages, shortly after Matt Conley's accident back in early January, and when Dan had checked four weeks ago. There was no traceable cause, nothing to show for it. Sam omitted to mention the cross, which, for a variety of reasons, was turning into a secret.

The time was two o'clock in the afternoon. Sam stopped the tractor and both men climbed out. After the drumming of the diesel engine the peace and quiet in the proximity of the Pot was noticeable.

'Quite pleasant along here,' Fred remarked.

'It's seen a lot of courting,' Sam replied.

'Not half,' Fred said with a meaningful nod of his head.

Sam pushed a way through the undergrowth and held back branches for Fred's benefit. They emerged almost together on the edge of the Pot and saw that it was full. The water was back where it had always been, darkly crystalline and still.

Sam exclaimed: 'Bless my soul!' – and recoiled, retreated a step, in a movement that verged on the melodramatic. 'I saw it empty with my own eyes, Fred. Who's playing tricks on us? Would Steve Judson do a thing like that, could he do it?'

'He got no spring water on his land – my answer's no.'

'You see how queer it is, Fred? Our Dan, he won't believe it. Nor will Nell.'

They checked the channel where water trickled again. They looked into Judson's field, and sought signs of digging by human or animal agencies along the cart track. Nothing was disturbed – even Judson's dry stone wall had been mended. They returned to the Pot, and Sam sat down on a tree stump while Fred lit one of his cheroots.

'Know what Nell's going to say? She'll say it's witch-work. She been on about witches since this all started.'

'I know bitches, I don't know witches,' Fred said with a smirk.

'There's Irish Maggie down Sheep Street.'

'What would old Maggie want with your water?'

'I don't know. I don't know nothing. Would have cost me if I'd had to pipe water into Big Field – somebody nasty could have wished me harm.'

'Who would that be?'

'You never can tell, that's the honest truth.'

'I've another question,' Fred began.

'What's that?'

'Where did the jewellery come from?'

'Jewellery? No jewellery that I've heard of. Where you get the story?'

'Your Nell was talking to my Glenys. She said it was found on your farm.'

'It's the Duke's farm. Nell tells fibs, they're in her mind – I'll straighten her out as soon as we're home. Nobody's found nothing that's the property of the Duke, not to my knowledge, Fred. And I'll thank you not to say otherwise.'

'You can trust me, Sam.'

Fred Croggett made an arrangement with Sam Iles to return the gearbox of the other farm tractor in seven or eight days, and drove his pick-up back to his business premises and residence.

Croggett's Cars was a dump. It was a used car lot, a scrap heap, an extensive garage and tool shed, a few petrol pumps and two rundown houses. It was also a local eyesore and the thorn in the flesh of successive local councillors of every political persuasion. Swearwords frequently described it; activists and do-gooders tried to wipe it off the face of the earth; the law was meant to get rid of it; yet it had survived for thirty-odd years. It just survived, it kept its nose above water, thanks first to Fred's slippery charm, then to bribery and corruption, then because it was useful, and lastly because it was unique. The uses of *Croggett's Cars* were that it could mend almost anything on wheels, and cheaper than any other establishment; its cars for sale were cut-price, too; it was a retirement home for mechanical write-offs, kaput fridges and dangerous cookers – it was a sort of public convenience. The uniqueness of Fred and his encampment was the other protective factor. Threats of visits, notices of appointments, summonses, final warnings and injunctions rained down on him, but his perennial response was masterly inactivity. He did not attend hearings in court, or pay fines, or clear up his act, and no bureaucrat had so far had the nerve to put him in prison and offend all the farmers who depended on his services, or to circumscribe his activities and provoke his numerous friends, mistresses and children in the neighbourhood.

Fred himself was made of some uniquely resistant matter. He was unmoved by, he rose above, every assault that might have done damage to the peace of mind of himself, his extended family and his clients. He lived in a state of anarchy and happy-go-lucky squalor on the edge of disaster – in practical terms, in one of his two houses with a son or grandson called Billy, aged eighteen, while Glenys shared the other house with temporary lovers, a teenage daughter, Marilyn, and the afore-mentioned Rose.

Numerous offspring of Fred, and their mothers for that matter, had come and gone over the years. He was impervious. He had urges, but purer emotions, fidelity, family feeling and tender memories, were not his pigeon. Glenys was thirty-five, a dyed blonde running to fat who was supposed to do office work for Fred at irregular hours. Her daughter Marilyn spent too much time in Chipping Sodbury and had already found herself briefly in the family way. The one exception in the history of Fred as paterfamilias was Rose.

He noticed her soon after she was born. He even spoke to her later on. He had time for her. He had never been so nice to any of his other descendants. She turned the tables on him, for, from the earliest age, she managed in a perfectly proper fashion to seduce the seducer. She was pretty enough, a little blonde elf usually with oil stains on her face and clothes; but it was her bold and affectionate personality that twanged heartstrings he had never before known he possessed.

In the afternoon of the day of his visit to Sodbury Holding he was greeted by Rose, who had been waiting for him amongst the corpses of cars. She had a pet name for him: once he had volunteered the endearment Ducky, and she had echoed it and always used it thereafter.

'Where you bin, Ducky?' she asked him. 'What we doing?'

He said he had to see a man about a dog.

'Don't go, Ducky. Look at my dolly.'

She thrust at him the doll, which had oil in its yellow hair.

He admired it and said: 'You find your Ma or go and play with Billy. Run along, love.'

He unloaded the gearbox and drove his pick-up down the road to Chipping Sodbury and on to Yate.

In Yate he turned off the Bristol road and eventually stopped in a back street outside a nondescript terrace house, clearly jerry-built in the '60s.

He knocked on the plywood front door with small window inset. After a pause, during which he spat out the wet stub of one cheroot and lit another, a face appeared in the window or spyhole, chains were released, locks turned, and the door was opened by a pale-faced, almost bald middle-aged man with bright blue eyes and a beaming smile. He was Harry Hailes, bachelor, horologist, that is clock-mender, gardener, also, discreetly, dealer in ill-gotten objects of value, and pawnbroker. He was considered a learned man in his small circle. It was also agreed generally that he was a terrible talker and that you had to pay a surcharge of patience for his services.

'Frederick Croggett, our friend Fred, how do you do?' Harry exclaimed, extending a hand, which Fred shook after wiping his own hand on the seat of his overall. 'Come in quick – we don't want to make a spectacle of ourselves, do we? Come into my parlour, as the spider said – or is it the workroom that would suit this afternoon?'

They moved into the workroom, a glory-hole of clocks ticking and striking, of chests and cabinets with multiple drawers, of a brightly lit work-bench in the window, and rows of instruments and tools on the walls.

Fred had to listen to a monologue on the culture of vegetables in Harry's allotment before a question was fired at him without any preamble or change of tone or facial expression.

'What is it today?'

'Something for you to look at, Harry.'

'Good of you to think of me – every little means a lot – my tastes are modest but have to be paid for – man was born to suffer, wasn't he, Fred?'

Fred cut through the verbiage: 'How much?'

'Time to look at something for you – nine plus one in the hand, if you please.'

Fred separated a tenner from a wad of notes withdrawn from some inner garment.

Harry launched into another welter of words, as Fred secreted his wad and searched deeper into a different pocket of his trousers and extracted an object wrapped in newspaper and a rubber band.

He laid it on the work-bench and Harry in his own time, after more smiles and references to his potatoes and suchlike, undid it and uncovered the object from Hetty's Pot.

'Legal, Fred?' he asked with his beatific smile.

'Paid for,' Fred replied.

'How much?'

'Too much for them marbles.'

'It's a cross.'

'Tell me another, Harry.'

'A Christian cross, I shouldn't wonder.'

'Are they glass?'

'They're stones.'

'What sort?'

Harry pointed to the central large stone in the 'vertical' strip of metal, the one between the two on the left and the two on the right of the 'horizontal' strip, and said: 'That's amethyst or I'm a Dutchman.'

'What's the one under, the green?'

'Don't rightly know. But here's a garnet, and this yellow's a citrine.' He had pointed to the stones on the extreme right of the 'horizontal' and on the left of the amethyst. 'They're precious stones, though they may be called semi-precious. I'd be interested to know what the seller thought they were. But I'm not nosey, Fred – wouldn't keep body and soul together if I was. All the same, no harm in saying you probably bought a bargain.'

'Put a price on it, Harry.'

'There are prices and prices, as well you know, Frederick. If I was buying it from you I'd offer eight hundred pounds.'

'Fancy that! You made me happy.'

'What'd you say to eight fifty?'

'I'd say sorry.'

'Oh well, can I offer you a drop in the spirit of friendship!'

'No, ta, Harry. You think I'll take five hundred after drinking your drops. You've given me what I was after. By the bye, if you was selling my cross in Bristol what price would you be looking for?'

'Bristol's a grand place, very grand, not like Yate.'

Fred winked and said, 'Point taken,' retrieved his property and slipped out of Harry's house with minimum delay.

In the tied bungalow at the back of the milking shed of Sodbury Holding, Dan and Peggy Green had been putting their marriage together again. Neither of them dwelt on their exchange of blows, they were not articulate people, and really worked too hard to take a few bruises to heart. The miscarriage had not injured Peggy, and she had already permitted Dan another shot at making a baby – in the cramped dimensions of their double bed there was no alternative to the love she aroused. At her insistence, he ceased to recapitulate the sequence of events at Hetty's Pot and to bother her with mystical notions. Now they were both pleased to have a mite of extra money in the bank.

They resumed their daily round. But Nell Palmer was inquisitive as well as superstitious, and her questions upset Peggy.

She asked if the cross was kept in a safe place.

'That it is, and private too,' Peggy replied.

Again, when Peggy cleaned the farmhouse one Saturday morning, Nell inquired: 'Why did you lose your baby?'

'I don't know, I'm sure – and that's that.'

Nell on a later occasion tried to establish a link between Matt Conley's accident, the water in the Pot, and the miscarriage.

'Did you ever think you might have been

part of all that?'

Peggy replied stoutly: 'Course not!'

Nell then pursued the matter.

'Sometimes I'm thinking we ought to call in the vicar, just in case. Would you object to having a word with a vicar, Peg?'

Peg objected. She had had a chat with the Reverend Timbrill at Lower Sodbury before her wedding – it had brought her out in heat bumps due to embarrassment.

'I'm not chatting to nobody,' she said. 'What happened to me is nature, and I'll keep it to myself if you don't mind.'

Unfortunately the poison was the slow kind. Although Peggy boasted to Dan that she had 'seen off' Nell, she began to brood and wonder if 'funny business', the supernatural in other words, could be to blame for everything. Soon she worried that she was somehow culprit rather than victim, and had done wrong to sell the cross – sell it in secret and against the wishes of her husband who had given it to her.

Perhaps Dan knew better: could a cross have the power he had talked about? Had it dished out punishment by influencing Dan to thump her and cause the loss of their baby? Motherhood promised her more pain than pleasure, but she would always be sorry to have gone and lost her first child.

Peggy could not understand, and was the more fearful the less she understood. She woke in the middle of her customary eight hours of heavy sleep, and lay there sweating and foreseeing accidents on purpose that were queueing up to happen to her.

Yet she was practical even in her panic, and arrived at the idea that the harm done might be undone. She could try to retract the sale and buy back the cross. The hundred and fifty pounds were intact and in an account in the Greens' joint names: each of them had the right to withdraw more or less money as required. To pinch Dan's share could be risky, but another row with him was a small price to pay for security in future and the safety of herself and her babies.

She heard that Fred Croggett was returning the tractor gearbox on such and such a day, and reported sick to her employers in the morning of the day in question.

At nine o'clock Fred arrived in his pick-up and parked in the farmyard. She was prepared and beckoned him. He saw her, scented trouble, nodded at her and turned away as if to deal with the gearbox. She ran across and caught him by the sleeve.

'Sorry, Mr Croggett, but I want a word so bad – only a minute, Mr Croggett – please come with me!'

He yielded to her, cursing himself for yielding to women and saying, 'Steady now! What's on offer today?'

By the garden gate of the bungalow, out of sight of anybody in the farmyard, Peggy let go of his sleeve and pleaded: 'Mr Croggett, can I have my cross back? I made a mistake. I'll pay all you paid me.'

'Sorry, Peggy – can't and won't – that's flat.'

'Why not?'

'You couldn't afford it, because it ran me into expenses when it was mine.'

'How much more than you paid me would you sell it for?'

'There's a better reason why. I can't – isn't mine no longer.'

'Honest?'

'I'm always honest, love.'

'Oh, you fibber!'

'Now now!'

'Mr Croggett, could I buy it from the person you sold it to?'

'What you want with a thing like that?'

'I think it was the death of my baby – on account of my selling it.'

'That's a load of nonsense.'

'I don't know what it'll do to us next.'

'A cross can't do nothing – you're talking wild – who's filled your head with stupid nonsense?'

'I'm frightened, Mr Croggett.'

'Don't be, love! You've no cause to be. Take my word for it! That cross won't do you any mischief, see?'

'You'll be worried too, Mr Croggett, if you're wrong by any chance.'

'Worried? I never worry, never have, not given that way. And don't you worry neither! I'm telling you true.'

'Thank you, Mr Croggett, though you won't help me.'

'You don't need my help, Peggy.'

'Maybe not,' she half-agreed, then, when he was walking away from her, she called after him: 'But maybe you'll be needing help one of these days.'

Fred had been a hard man, although his voice was soft and his shallow bonhomie and reputation persuaded lots of women to give him whatever he wanted. But the passage of time and a granddaughter were changing his nature. A simile culled from his type of work was applicable to him: he was like a worn car tyre with a slow puncture.

Having delivered that gearbox to Sam Iles and fitted it, he drove back towards *Croggett's Cars*, thinking of Peggy Green. He was sorry for her. Strangely enough, he was not only sorry, he regretted something not very nice he had done. He could not have brought himself to tell her the true truth – he would have been in danger of kissing goodbye at least seven hundred pounds. He had paid one fifty for the cross, Harry Hailes valued it at eight fifty – the difference meant a healthy profit, and it would have been sick of him to return it to Peggy for damn all.

Fred Croggett was a professional purveyor of inaccuracy – he was not in the secondhand car business for nothing; but he was not happy to have stood there lying in the face of Peggy Green – 'poor stupid cow', as he described her to himself. She was poor and stupid in his opinion to imagine that a little cross with a bit missing could do damage or have any effect to speak of on anything. Yet why had he told her not to worry? How could he be sure she had no reason to worry? An uncharacteristic query lurked at the back of his mind: was he the stupid one to have bought the cross in the first place and in the second to have conned and misled its previous owner?

He arrived at *Croggett's Cars* and entered the big shed. Billy was there, under a car, but he wriggled out and, lying on his back on the oily concrete, spoke to his father.

'Glenys wants you. Rosie's back from hospital.'

'What's that?'

'A bumper fell off and dropped on her.'

'Is she bad?'

'Broke ribs, they told Glenys.'

Fred blushed, he could feel the blood rush to his head, he remembered Peggy's warning and jumped to the conclusion that the cross was getting its own back for his bad behaviour.

He hurried to his house, removed his overall and washed his hands thoroughly – he never liked to lay grubby hands on Rose or soil her in any way, and now was taking special care. Then he crossed to Glenys' house and walked in. Rose was in the sitting room, wearing her nightie and dressing-gown, and with the blanket from her cot with its design of rabbits thrown over her. She was surrounded by toys, the TV was showing a cartoon, and Glenys must have been out the back.

Rose's blue eyes showed signs of tears, she had been grizzling, and at the sight of Fred her mouth turned down and she began to whimper and cry.

He knelt down and stroked her forehead.

'Oh please, stop it hurting, Ducky,' she gulped out.

'What have they done to you, pet?' he asked.

'Took me to hospital.'

'They'll make you better soon.'

'Will I die, Ducky?'

'No fear! You'll be yourself in next to no time.'

'Ow, ow!'

'Hurts when you cry, love, hurts when you breathe – better try to be still.'

'I can't – ow!'

Glenys appeared and said at once to her father: 'Those old cars piled one on top of another aren't safe – bloody bumper might have done for her.'

'I'll move them out tomorrow,' he said.

'That's a story I've heard before. Why can't we live in a tidy place like other people? They've given her pills to send her sleepy.'

'Any danger?'

'Not if she keeps warm and breathes normal. Let her sleep now, Pa.'

He addressed Rose: 'I'll be off so that you can get better quicker.'

Rose turned her head away, whether to show displeasure or because of the pain.

'It's for your good, love,' he said, and tiptoed towards the door.

To Glenys he said sorry and asked her to tell him how Rose fared during the day. Out of doors he did not know what to do with himself. He was badly shaken. He had thoughts in his head that might have been called religious. He was an atheist with knobs on, a heathen from top to bottom; but he wished Rose to be cured, and even he had a hazy idea that wishes were prayers.

Back in his own house he donned his overall again and then had another look at the cross. That such a small object had any power over people was preposterous. He rolled it up in its newspaper and resumed work alongside Billy in the shed.

Rose slept for hours. She was still sleeping when Fred shut up shop at six o'clock in the evening. In his own house he sat down for five minutes, intending to have another wash and brush-up before supper with Glenys. He was anxious and tired – phenomena with which he was unacquainted. First Peggy had got him down, then Rose upset him, and for once he felt guilty, and that he should be doing more for someone else than he had done, today or ever. He nearly dropped into a nightmarish doze, but resisted and struggled to his feet for Rose's sake. The ring of the doorbell was like an electric shock – he assumed it was bad news.

It rang again. He took a deep breath and opened the door. Not Glenys or Billy stood outside, but a red-haired woman, not young, coarse-looking, in a skimpy dress.

'Fred,' she said.

'What are you after?' he inquired in unwelcoming tones.

'Let me in, Fred – it's a cold evening.'

'Where's your coat?'

But he allowed her to float past him on a cloud of scent. The scent, her excess of lipstick and the dress were warning signals. He knew her inside out – she had been one of his women long ago.

'You're not stopping here, Ruby. My granddaughter's ill across the way. I'll give you a couple of minutes.'

'Okay, Fred. I need money.'

'You're not getting it from me.'

'Lend me.'

'None to spare, old girl.'

'I'll pay it back.'

'How's that?'

'Somehow.'

'Stale buns, Ruby.'

'Oh you are rude, Fred. You're rude and cruel, you are, like all men. Anything to drink?'

'Not for you.'

'Can I use your toilet?'

'If you must.'

She went upstairs, she knew the house, having lived in it once, and was back by the time he had discarded the chewed end of his cheroot and lit another.

In the doorway she paused, aimed a lubricious glance at him, extended a hand holding a red satin triangular-shaped apology for knickers and dangled them invitingly.

He averted his eyes. She was too old for it, and too fat and too predictable. The pathetic aspect of her was not an aphrodisiac, and even Fred's concupiscence drew the line at it. More negative still was the novel idea that a shot of routine sex would be considered offensive by the forces that might be able to mend little Rose.

Ruby sank down on one of the two easy

chairs, saying, 'You're not the man you were,' and burst into bitter and ugly tears.

'What's he done to you now?' Fred asked. He was referring to Eddy Wilmot, Ruby's latest.

'He wants money, more money, and I can't get it.'

'Still working, are you?'

'When somebody's willing, and that's not often.'

'Why not retire, Ruby, and get a straight job?'

'He won't let me, and I don't know nothing.'

'Well, it's a hard life. I've my grand-daughter to see to. And I may need money for her one way or other.'

'Nothing for me?'

'Sorry.'

'He'll kill me.'

'No! You're the goose that lays the golden eggs.'

'That goose got itself killed.'

'I wouldn't want you dead, not on top of what's on my shoulders already.' He produced his wad of notes and peeled one off. 'Take a twenty, but, remember, I'll kill you if you ask for more.'

'God bless you, Fred.'

'Hang on! God hasn't done a lot for you, Ruby.'

'It's not like that.'

'Do me a favour – put in a word for my Rose – you speak to God for me, will you?'

'I don't know religion, Fred.'

'Look, I'll make it worth your while.' He took the packet of newspaper off the mantelpiece and handed it to her. He told her to unwrap it.

She held the cross and asked: 'Is it valuable?'

'Worth a bob or two, but you keep hold of it for a rainy day.'

'Is it holy?'

'I don't know, I'm not saying, but it's yours – you do right by it and it'll do right by you.'

'It's more than I should have, Fred.'

'No – you take care of it – and do what you can for Rose.'

'Thanks, Fred. I will. Good luck, Fred. Ta-ta.'

He was alone again, and felt better in spite of wondering at himself for acting against his interests. He washed and so on, and walked over and into Glenys' house. She was in the kitchen, she was with Billy, and called to him to join them. He pushed open the sitting room door to check on Rose's state.

She saw him. She was awake. She looked well again, and was playing with her dolly in her dainty elfin way. She smiled at him and questioned as usual: 'Where you bin, Ducky?'

Pain in the Wallet

Ruby Simmons, formerly married to and divorced by Evan Davies and by Rick Johnson, had reverted to her maiden surname but not to the Christian names, Ethel Jane, by which she was baptised. Ruby was a slob, a slag and pretty much of a lost cause. She was worse than she should have been, more stupid that she ought to have become, as lazy in some ways as she was energetic in others, and altogether too kind and tolerant for her own good.

She hailed from Stroud. Her parents were rottenly respectable in the opinion of their rebellious red-haired Ethel Jane, aged fifteen, with her precocious physique and weakness for boys. She ran away from her conscientious newsagent father, her sharp-tongued mother and her jealous older sister, with the youth who worked the dodgems in a travelling fair. She was Ruby now, and fair game for men of all sorts and conditions. She drifted into two marriages, she drifted into divorce courts, she drifted into hospitals to give birth to her children, a boy and a girl – fathers not known for certain – who were soon surrendered for adoption.

She scarcely knew in the morning whose bed she would share in the night. She was not averse to living in Fred Croggett's dump. She was a piece of flotsam on a sea of sex.

To start with she got what she wanted, excitement, risky action, carefree fun and no regrets. Then she got what she had not wanted. She did not like to do some of the things she was reduced to doing. The other side of the medal of eating, drinking and being merry was a nagging kind of remorse. Her life kept on changing for the worse, and, while she waited in vain for it to change for the better, time passed relentlessly. She found herself on her own, and asking herself the common depressing question of middle age, 'What next?', when she met Edmund Wilmot, known as Eddy.

He admitted to being fifty-five. He was a tall man with flat black hair, and dressed smartly in double-breasted suits, collars and ties. They met in the pub significantly called The Sheep and Goats, standing beside the little-used link road between Lower Sodbury and Chipping. She formed the impression that he was a gentleman, he talked proper and had authority, and he found out that she lived alone in a council house on the outskirts of Chipping. He steered her into offering him a night's shelter, and impressed her further by not taking it for granted that copulation was included. He stayed on, he stayed put, and she did not like to object.

He was a conman, a small-time crook and gambler, and peculiar into the bargain. Ruby was prepared to pardon most male peccadillos, but Eddy's peculiarities were distressing. He rejected her offers of herself. He was not affectionate and shrank from physical contact. He slept on her settee, kept himself to himself, was a cut-price dandy and spent his spare time washing and ironing his clothes and shaving the frayed edges of his shirt-collars and cuffs. Money was sex for him, money was his god and be-all and end-all. That he seldom had any money, and never hung on to the money he did have, was the basis of his touch of pathos.

The manner he affected was military – he claimed to have served in the SAS, the Irish Guards, the Gloucesters and other regiments, depending on who he was talking to and which pub he was in. He imitated the starchy sergeant-major type, or even the fire-eating colonel, but then he would laugh disarmingly, act dignity in defeat, pull a face, giggle, and win a degree of popularity as stern schoolmasters do by suddenly showing they are human after all.

He was altogether a fantasist. He seemed to believe he had been a distinguished officer, and was irresistible to women; when in fact he did not seduce women, he quelled them, and he was no better than a pimp. In the early days Ruby had been taught a disagreeable lesson. She ventured to show a flicker of curiosity verging on irritability: she asked him if he was queer or something. He began by enumerating the reasons why she did not attract him, listed her double chin, drooping breasts, protuberant stomach and so on, and ended equally mercilessly by twisting her arm behind her back and giving it a jerk that meant it was out of action for three months.

Afterwards he apologised. He wished her to know that he had the greatest respect for members of the weaker sex. He assured her that nothing of the sort would happen again, provided he was not provoked beyond bearing. But he could have saved his breath: once was enough for Ruby, she feared as well as hating and pitying him.

What was she to do?

Her answer to this repetitive question was always the same. She had no alternative. Rescue was part of her dream that did not and probably never would come true. Her days of thinking she could treat men badly were long gone. Now the men who desired her treated her like a public lavatory, and the others only wanted to be pals. She had no confidence that she could do better than

Eddy, and she dreaded loneliness. She could not manage on her own, she was made for family life but had affronted her destiny, and the prospect of a future with nobody, with nothing, without orders to obey, shopping to buy, someone to cook for, and company in the evening, drained away the meagre residue of her energy and courage.

On the evening of her call on Fred Croggett, Eddy had given her the exact money to pay for two gallons of petrol for his ancient Mini – he was going to the races on the next day. She bought the petrol and was overcome by misery and hunger. She had no money, not a penny, and there was no food at home, and she could not face yet another evening at The Sheep, where he would not buy her anything to eat, she would have to beg, borrow and scrounge in order to feed herself and provide him with food, drink and cash to fritter away on sure things at Newbury.

She drove home via a convenience store in Old Sodbury. She spent five of the twenty pounds Fred had given her on the cheapest foodstuffs, then stowed a flyer in her bag for Eddy to find and extract. A short distance from her cottage she stopped the car, got out, hid a tenner in her red knickers and the cross in its newspaper wrapping under stones in the wall alongside the dark road.

In the morning Ruby woke with a hangover and shied away mentally from remembering the previous evening. She postponed washing and threw on a well-worn dressing-gown: why should she bother with her appearance for Eddy? He was already up and about – one of his boasts was that he was never ill and would not knuckle under to illness anyway. He had drunk more than she had at The Sheep, she had had to drive the Mini home as best she could; but he was the most disciplined of utterly disorganised men. He polished his shoes and brushed his trilby, and provoked her by referring to their day out at Newbury for the umpteenth time.

'I've told you, Eddy, I'm staying put today.'

'Why is that, my dear?' he asked.

'You know perfectly well.'

'Remind me.'

'I've loose covers to finish for Mrs Ford.'

'You prefer upholstery to my company.'

'What are you talking about? I've told you over and over again that I have work to do.'

'I'm extremely offended.'

'Eddy, Mrs Ford pays me, you don't pay me for watching you at the races lose the money I make.'

He laughed, he giggled loosely and said: 'Too true! I don't pay people for having a good time with me. But why suggest I'm going to lose money?' His tone changed: 'I take that amiss, Ruby. You seem to want me to lose money. You must do better than that. Come on, I'm listening!'

'Win for me, Eddy – come back loaded!'

'If I do lose, you'll be in trouble. Don't forget it – will you, dear?'

At last she was rid of him. She was exhausted by the argument that was nearly a quarrel he had typically picked, and her head ached. She was not in the mood, or strong enough, to concentrate on Mrs Ford's loose covers, although upholstery was her financial lifeline. She tidied her bed and lay down on it.

Memories barged into her brain – she could not keep them out. Evenings at pubs, and in particular at The Sheep, the drinking, the begging, the lies and the sex, all was unthinkable; but now she could not stop thinking of it. No part of the rigmarole was censored by her wishes. Yesterday evening Eddy with Ruby in tow had arrived at The Sheep at seven and stayed until eleven. Eddy had shot his lines to a well-heeled gent – orphan, Barnardo boy, war hero, down on his luck; to a gullible old woman from the village – he would put her pennies on a wonder horse at Newbury; to a half-cut chum – loan, please; and to landlord Les – he would pay his debt some time never. How embarrassing it was! How badly those drinks disagreed with her!

And then the muttered exchanges between Eddy and Tom, Dick or Harry made her heart sink at the time and her conscience torment her afterwards!

Yesterday it was Tom in person, a crude farmboy from Tormarton way, who paid Eddy money for her services.

'Ruby, you're acquainted with Tom, aren't you? Have a chat with him – he's dead set on having a chat. Be kind, Ruby – no harm in kindness!'

Les was paid too for handing over the key to the hut in the garden with the mattress on the floor and cushions, towels and tissues. Ruby never mentioned a fee, she would only refer to the generosity of her clients, and often as a result got nothing except a rude rebuff – 'I'm not paying twice over, see?' As for Tom, he gave her nothing much of any description, no satisfaction, and one pound in small change. The best compliment she could have paid him, if compliments had figured in their inarticulate exchange, was that he did not hang about.

When would it, how could it, end?

She surrendered to despair and loathing of herself. Escapism, restlessness, took hold of her. Work was out of the question. She left the house, looked carefully to right and left, for Eddy was capable of waiting to pounce upon her and drive her back to the treadmill of earning his keep, crossed the road, and again after taking precautions lifted a stone in the roadside wall and felt underneath.

The package was still there. She had slipped into a shirt and a skirt, and now she reached under her skirt and stuffed the package into her knickers. It was preposterous at her age that she should have to hide things in her knickers, but where else would be safe from Eddy's intrusiveness? She walked up the road and climbed over a gate into a wood. There was a ride through the wood, and she followed it, then diverged through undergrowth and came to a fallen oak tree, its barkless trunk white with age, and sat down.

She and the fallen tree were old friends. Sitting on it, hidden from Eddy and the rest of the world, had occasionally cured some of her ills. She was sure she could commit suicide safely in that sequestered place and not be found for days. But suicide was another dream – she knew she lacked the nerve to do it.

She reached for and unwrapped her package. Beams of wintry sun, mote-filled in the windless weather, shone down on her and seemed to be caught in the coloured stones of the little cross. She held it in one hand and stroked it with the other, and her morbid thoughts receded. She contemplated the object exclusively, admired it,

67

turned it this way and that, loved it, and was grateful to Fred Croggett.

The cross was the best thing she had – and had had for years. It was the most beautiful, the only beautiful thing she had ever possessed. She was as unmaterialistic as Eddy Wilmot was avaricious, yet she realised that its value, the bob or two that Fred had said it was worth, might give her the power to liberate herself and live a better life, if she dared. She knew enough about money to know that without it freedom was virtually out of reach. And she had learned the hard way that Eddy was controllable by nothing but cash.

The cross let her break rules. It sanctioned the indulgence of dreaming of her children, Joe and Jenny: as a rule she kept them at arm's length, in a manner of speaking, in case they stole up on her and broke her heart. One day would she, might she really, have the money and the will to try to trace them – not to interfere or divide their loyalties between their adoptive mothers and their natural one, just to be sure they were well and happy?

But Fred had warned her not to fool around with the cross, and she made up her mind never to sell it except in emergency. That meant, in her own words, she was back to square one. There was no money in the offing, and the reality was more grinding on, more ratcheting down, with the man she dreaded and despised. On the other hand, more positively, the cross had at least extended the line of her horizon.

She wrapped it in its newspaper, hid it first in her knickers, then in the stone wall, and returned home.

It was the middle of the day; Eddy was still absent, and she was sure she had not been watched or seen.

The telephone rang and scared her.

She was afraid to answer. It must be bad news – Eddy would not pay to use public telephones, and almost no one else rang. He could have been taken ill, and she would be saddled with an invalid. But she could not restrain a pang of pity for him, and therefore had to hear the worst, whatever it was. She picked up the instrument and said with brash bravado: 'Yes?'

A man spoke – a deep voice she did not recognise – polite, hesitant – asking a question.

'I wonder if you could help me – I'm searching for a relative – does the name Ethel mean anything to you?'

'Who are you?'

'Ethel Jane Simmons?'

'What do you want?'

'Do you happen to know a lady of that name, or know of her?'

'That depends. What's your game?'

'It's no game, madam. My name is Joseph Davies...'

Ruby dropped the telephone. She had been standing in the kitchen, and now her legs gave way under her and she sank down on the vinyl tiles. Perhaps she fainted briefly, then she was surprised by awareness of alternately burning with heat and freezing, and by a voice repeating over and over again: 'Hullo? Hullo? Are you all right? Hullo, are you all right?'

She picked up the instrument and held it to her ear laboriously.

'Are you Joe?' she asked.

'Are you Ethel Jane Simmons?'

'Yes and no. Are you my son?'

'What does "no" mean?'

'I've changed my name. I was married to Evan Davies once, and had his child, a boy. It was years ago.'

'I'm thirty-seven. You're my mother. I've looked for you for a long long time.'

'Oh God!'

'I'm afraid I've shocked you. Forgive me! I found out that you called yourself Ruby, but I couldn't believe that you would be the right Ruby.'

'I'm the one that needs forgiving. I did so wrong by you, Joe, you and Jenny. I never have forgiven myself.'

'You were too young to know any differ-

70

ent. There's no hard feelings, none, on my side. I knew of your existence through the Parish Register in Stroud, but no more than that. Anyhow, it's the future I'm interested in, not the past.'

'Are you well, Joe?'

'Yes. Are you?'

'Don't let's speak about me. Are you happy?'

'Oh yes – married to a good wife – and we have four children, your grandchildren.'

'What are their names?'

'Robert, he's ten, Billy who's eight, Sam, six, and Jane, four – we called her Jane because of you. I've got a decent job in printing, and Grace, my wife, she works part time as receptionist in a doctors' practice.'

'How wonderful!'

'Well, I'd second that.'

'And strange, Joe, strange – I was thinking of you only half an hour ago – I've thought of you so many times, but today was special.'

'That's another coincidence – there's been enough coincidences to fill a book, let alone get us to the point of talking together. We live far from where you are, we're east of you, in Essex, but I sometimes come your way on business and we could meet.'

'No!'

'Grace would like to meet you too, and the children. Would you prefer to come our way?'

'No, no, I can't.'

'Have I said something wrong? I'm sure this must be upsetting for you – it is for me, but happy too.'

'I can't see you.'

'Oh...'

'Try to understand. It's more than happy for me. But I haven't led a good life, Joe. I'd be ashamed for you to see me as I am. Oh, Joe, these things are so hard to say!'

'I'm sorry. Shall I ring another day?'

'No – please – don't go!'

'Can I ask if you live alone?'

'Yes, you can, and no, I don't – I live with Eddy Wilmot – I'm not married to him or anything.'

'Is he good to you?'

'I wouldn't like you to meet him, Joe.'

'Oh dear! Are you hard up?'

'You mustn't give me money – your money's for your family.'

'What am I to call you?'

'I'm not Ethel any more, and I don't want to be called by my other name.'

'What about Mother?'

'I don't deserve it, but... But I'd love that, Joe.'

'As you know, I have your telephone number and your address.'

'They're in the phone book for you or Jenny – no other reason – I don't phone people often, and people don't phone me –

I kept Simmons in the book just in case.'

'May I ring you again?'

'Yes. Oh yes – but please don't believe anything Eddy tells you if you get through to him.'

'Have you got a pencil handy? Here's my number.'

He reeled it off and she wrote it down.

'Listen,' he said. 'I'm hoping you'll meet me – take your time and change your mind if possible. The people who adopted me were lovely. They're no longer with us, sad to say. I've been so lucky that I couldn't judge the unlucky ones. I wouldn't interfere or try to boss you about. If we could be friends, great, but I'm quite ready to accept that we might have to agree to go our separate ways. I'm not attaching strings to this conversation, and I wouldn't to a meeting.'

'Joe... Joe... Ring me when I can talk without crying.'

'I will, Mother, I promise I will.'

Ruby spent the next four hours in an emotional storm. She had fits of crying and loss of all control. She had spasms of unwonted joy and optimism. She lay on her bed. She could not be still. Her world was filled with brightness until the black clouds representing Eddy's return gathered and approached.

He arrived at seven o'clock. He had won at Newbury, he must have won a large sum of money, for he gave Ruby twenty pounds for housekeeping. He was in a good mood and boasted of his fail-safe method of betting. He noticed nothing amiss, and sat at the kitchen table, waiting for his supper.

As she tried to serve his egg, sausage, tomatoes and chips, her hand began to shake and she dropped her palette knife on the floor.

'What's got into you?' he demanded.

She cried again.

He fired more questions at her, and eventually she felt forced to answer.

'My son rang me today.'

'What are you talking about?'

'My son Joe rang me.'

'What for? Did he curse you for giving him up?'

'Not at all. It was so nice. It was the best thing that's ever happened to me.'

'Why are you crying then?'

'For goodness sake, Eddy!'

'I won't have no one making you cry.'

'He wants to meet me.'

'I'm not standing for that.'

'It's not your business. It's nothing to do with you.'

'We'll see. Did he beg for money?'

'Oh Eddy, no – he's not like you.'

'Is that so? Thank you, my dear. Where's he been all these years if he's so nice? Why did he leave it to me to protect you? Does he

know what you've been up to? I could give
him the hot news.'

'You wouldn't!'

'Why not? I don't want him muscling in
on my patch.'

'I'd kill you, Eddy.'

He stood up abruptly – china fell on the
floor – he was beside her, holding her arm
with one hand and squeezing her neck with
the other.

'Like to try?'

He repeated the question.

She freed herself sufficiently to say: 'Stop
it or I'll tell my son.'

He let her go at once.

'I'll tell my son if you ever hurt me again,
Eddy.'

He laughed. He retreated to his chair, sat
down, looked at her in a crestfallen way and
giggled. He seemed to subside and shrink
into half the man he had been, and he
giggled as if to excuse himself.

Ruby's mind was made up. She could never
meet Joe. Her shame was one reason why,
and Eddy was another. From a mother's
point of view she could see herself in lurid
colours, and Eddy was untrustworthy, and
had the power to blackmail her or ruin her
chances to be part of a normal family. She
could not bear to disappoint her son on top
of having rejected him.

At the same time she took certain steps that seemed to be preparatory. She had her hair cut shorter and decided to let the red dye grow out: brown hair with grey showing through was her new preference. She wore a bra again and dressed more respectably in darker clothes. She finished Mrs Ford's loose covers and worked on other overdue upholstery jobs. The money she earned enabled her to refuse a couple of requests for private 'chats' in the garden shed at the Sheep and Goats. She drank less, trying to prove that she was not an alcoholic, and ate with a view to losing weight.

Three weeks passed without a word from Joe, and Ruby's confidence slumped. Her pessimism took over, and her negative passivity. Yet she did her best not to leave the house, she waited in principle to say no.

Joe rang one evening when Eddy had gone to the pub. Ruby spoke to him breathlessly.

After the preamble he said: 'It's Thursday today, and on Saturday we'd all like to take you out to lunch. We could meet beside the clock in Chipping Sodbury's High Street – I've read about the clock. Would you meet us there, Mother? Could you get there at twelve noon?'

'Yes,' she swallowed and replied. 'Yes, I'd love to, thank you so much, Joe. You're sure it's not too far for you? Thank you, thank you.'

Much later that same evening Eddy returned home, slightly tipsy. Ruby's nerves were strained to breaking point by then, and she immediately broached the awkward subject.

'My Joe has asked me to have lunch and meet his wife and children on Saturday.'

'Oh?'

'At Chipping Sodbury.'

'Indeed?'

'I've said I'd be there.'

'What time are we expected?'

'Eddy... Sorry, I'm going alone. I haven't seen Joe for thirty-seven years – it's bound to be a strain for both of us – I couldn't cope in front of you.'

'I see.'

'That probably means you don't see.'

'I thought you might like a shoulder to cry on.'

'Thanks... But sorry... Please let me go, don't make it difficult.'

'My intentions were good, Ruby, and you've proved once more the road to hell is paved with good intentions. Keep your date and good luck to you! I'm tired and want to lie down.'

It had been better than she feared, and worse – she hated his act of dignity in distress. He teased her, he tortured her, by behaving meekly on the next day; and on the Saturday morning he offered to drive her into Chipping Sodbury. She let him, she took pity on him, her suspicions notwithstanding – besides, she had not fancied the walk from Old Sodbury to Chipping.

All began badly. Eddy delayed their departure. Ruby grew angry as well as nervous, and foresaw the mortifying scene in store. Joe and his family were already under the clock. Greetings were constrained, the more so on her side because she had to introduce Eddy, whose grim military manners made her wish he was dead. Then Joe invited Eddy to join in the lunch. He accepted, Ruby had to tell him to get lost, everybody was embarrassed, and Eddy managed to put his spanner in the works.

He said: 'I'll thank you to take note, Joe Davies, that your mother's no angel from heaven – and I can supply chapter and verse, should you ever be interested.'

He stalked off. She cried. Joe put his arm round her shoulders, Grace produced a clean tissue, the children watched wide-eyed. After a brief matrimonial exchange, Joe led his mother away and down a side-street to the church and a seat under yew trees in the graveyard.

She confessed as her sobs decreased: 'I've done everything bad except drugs, but I'm not a bad person, not on purpose, honestly. It's been one mistake after another – leaving you and Jenny and making a fool of myself

78

without stopping – and Eddy Wilmot's the latest, and he's the last. I must tell you, before he does – I don't want you to think I'm as good as I wish I had been.'

He comforted her. He was dark-haired and rosy-cheeked, slim built like his father. She loved him more than she had loved other men, if differently; she believed she could trust him.

As they walked back to rejoin the rest of the family in the Queen's Hotel, she said: 'You are my angel from heaven,' and he laughed at her and dismissed it.

Grace kissed Ruby then, and Ruby kissed the children. They ate lunch and talked, talked with increasing ease, and carried on talking over coffee in the lounge. At some stage the oldest child Robert and the three younger ones led Ruby out to the car park to show her the nodding dogs visible through the rear window of the family car. On their return, Joe took the children to the shops, leaving Ruby and Grace alone.

'We fixed it so that you and I could put our heads together,' Grace said with her nice wide smile.

'I've lots to tell you,' she continued. 'Joe didn't like to spill any beans before I'd met you. Now we have met, I can ask if you'd like to come and live in a house of ours not too near or too far from where we live. Don't speak yet! Joe's feelings for you are emotional, but he's always had and always will have them. My attitude's realistic, and I'm hoping you'll understand me. I need help with the children. Grandmother Trench, the survivor of the couple who adopted Joe, died not long ago – she was there for me and for us until she went into hospital. My parents are miles away, and I don't want to leave my children with strangers. Now Joe's getting a more important job and we'll be travelling abroad. Are you interested? How committed are you to Eddy Wilmot? I don't know you by ordinary standards, but I think I do know you by standards of my own. And we could be on approval to each other. Money's no problem.'

In the course of the next hour or two Ruby's life was reordered. Obstacles were negotiated, difficulties overcome, details dealt with, arrangements and dates fixed. Joe would telephone on the Friday evening of the week ahead to check that he could drive over and fetch her on the Saturday.

At four o'clock she was dropped back at her cottage, and she waved and was waved goodbye by the magical family of which she was soon to be a permanent member.

Eddy's reaction to her news was not violent. He was nonchalant and haughty to start with, and in the ensuing days sulky when sober, and self-pitying after evenings at the Sheep. But he giggled when she tried to discuss his future, and gave her extra reasons to fear that he would come to grief without her. He had ceased to iron his suits and polish his shoes, and, by accident or design, showed even less gumption than usual.

Ruby served notice that she would be vacating her cottage and recommended Eddy Wilmot to the local Council. She urged Eddy to take on the tenancy – he would manage to pay his way with the Invalidity Benefit he had wangled and the Housing Benefit he was likely to receive. She apologised for deserting him, letting him down, not supplementing his income as she had done, and having no spare money to soften these blows. That she owed him nothing, that he had dragged her deeper into the dirt, did not minimise her guilt. In fact, the more she measured the extent of her luck, the sharper her conscience pricked her in respect of Eddy's misfortunes.

On the Friday before the Saturday when her new life was due to start, Ruby reached a tough decision. Early in the morning, while Eddy was still asleep in the front room, she interrupted the packing of her few possessions to slip out at the back and fetch the cross from its hiding place. In the afternoon, following a meal of sandwiches that Eddy ate in silence, she presented it to him with a little speech.

'Fred Croggett gave it to me. He said it would be good to me if I was good to it. Well, my dream's coming true, whether or not that's to do with the cross. But you be good to it, Eddy, and maybe it'll repay you. I've a funny feeling that it's more precious somehow or other than its money value.'

He thanked her. His gratitude was not rendered more acceptable by his giggling. But he fingered and studied the cross, and appeared to be pleased with it.

Later he drove her to the pub for the last time. It was packed with strangers – there had been an Antiques Fair in Bath and they were the antique dealers heading north on their way home. Eddy and Ruby immediately parted company: she was offered farewell drinks by the landlord, Les Holmes, and other regulars who knew her more or less well – the 'goat' Tom was one of them.

At about eight o'clock Eddy lurched over, leading by the hand a big old blonde, Deirdre by name, who was apt to pay men instead of being paid for 'chats' in the garden shed. He was slightly tipsy, but looking pleased with himself and in military mood.

'Ruby, I'll be staying with Deirdre tonight,' he slurred. 'I'm bowing out so your Joe won't trip over me. I thought you'd be relieved to know. You have nothing more to worry about – and thanks for the memory.'

Ruby was not particularly pleased. He turned on his heel, dragging after him Deirdre, who dared to smirk at her. Was that his goodbye?

Half an hour later he was buying champagne at the bar, one bottle, then another, and sending a glass of it across to herself, raising his own glass to her, and treating lots of unknown people to glasses. He was flushed and happier than she had ever seen him, laughing, not giggling, and not, as usual, morosely drunk.

She guessed that he had sold the cross, and was put out that he had ignored her advice. But if he was under Deirdre's wing, if he had money in his pocket for once, she would be generous, grudge nothing, and take pleasure in having achieved the best part of her object.

Another half hour elapsed, and Les beckoned and told her that Eddy was in trouble in the garden. She went out to him – he was bawling and boo-hooing. It was a dry night, he was hunched up on a garden seat in the semi-darkness, and he clung to her. She was horrified, and overwhelmed with mixed feelings.

'I'm so sorry,' she kept on saying, patting him on the back. She had thought him incapable of such strong emotion, and was afraid he would cut his throat for her sake or do something even worse.

'Please, Eddy, control yourself – you mustn't be sad – you never really loved me – you'll be better off with Deirdre.'

But he sobbed and retched and croaked: 'I'm done for.'

'No, you're not – you mustn't cry for me – I'm not worth it, Eddy.'

'I'm done for – I was done – lost... Lost!'

'What are you saying?'

'Sold your cross...'

'Oh, that! I know, I guessed, I don't mind, Eddy, I don't mind that.'

'I got a grand.'

'That's not bad. You're welcome to it.'

'But then...'

'What then?'

'Woman bought it... She bought it for five thousand... I was done. Four thousand!'

'Is that why you're crying, Eddy?'

'Four grand lost!'

She laughed at him or perhaps at herself.

'Don't,' he begged her. 'Don't laugh, Ruby. I'll never get over it. I'm a goner.'

'Where's your lady-love?'

'Getting car.'

'You go with Deirdre. I'll drive the Mini home and leave it there for you to collect. Poor Eddy! Silly Eddy! Silly me! Bye-bye!'

Crimes of Love

The woman who paid five thousand pounds for the cross was Melissa Proctor, wife of Giles Proctor. The Proctors were the proprietors of Baubles and Beads, a shop at the top end of Chipping Sodbury High Street that sold curios and antique jewellery. But Melissa bought the cross without the agreement of Giles, and neither for sound business reasons nor for profit, but to advance her very own cause of adultery.

In the bar of the Sheep and Goats, Eddy Wilmot had sold the cross to Mikey Solomon, an antique dealer from Cheltenham, and Mikey showed it to Carton Digby, the jeweller with a shop on the upper floor of a building in Bury Street, St James's. Carton was a grandee amongst traders in antiquities. He identified the stones in the cross, said it was an attractive item, but that it would not suit his somewhat irreligious clientele. Standing close to him at the time, perhaps closer than she should have stood, was Melissa Proctor.

She piped up to say she was interested.

Mikey Solomon knew her and her shop, and suggested in veiled terms that the price would be beyond her means, too high for Baubles and Beads to pay, and out of reach of the retail punters of Chipping Sodbury.

Carton looked at her with half-closed eyes, and taunted her by chiming in: 'You have been warned.'

'I won't be underestimated,' she cried with an excited mettlesome laugh. 'You're both trying to put me down. What do you want for the damn thing, Mikey?'

'More than you'd like to hear, my dear.'

'No – come on – don't tell me you're unwilling to make money!'

'Five big ones, and I'm advising you not to pay me.'

'Done!'

Carton said, 'No, Melissa–'

She interrupted him, she challenged him with shiny eyes and moist smile, 'Yes, Carton, yes!'

Amidst more laughter she rummaged in her bag, produced pen and chequebook, wrote the cheque on the Baubles and Beads account, and handed it to Mikey.

Shortly afterwards Carton said he would have to wend his way homewards, meaning to his house in the country in the direction of Iron Acton. He leant down to kiss Melissa goodbye. She prolonged it and whispered in his ear, 'Come and see me,' to which he replied in an undertone, 'Soon.'

Melissa then fetched Giles, who sat at the

bar consuming non-alcoholic drinks – they had agreed that he would do the driving to their home over the shop. She bade everyone good night in high-spirited and self-satisfied tones, and out of doors clamped her mouth shut and marched towards and into the passenger seat of the car aggressively.

They drove in silence for a mile or two.

Giles inquired: 'Had a nice time, Melissa dear?'

How she hated him! How clever he was at infuriating her!

'Extremely nice.'

'You must forgive me,' he resumed. 'I had no idea that you were such a religious woman. If I'd known I would have dragged you to church twice on Sundays.'

'There are many things you don't know about me.'

'True! Was Carton in good form this evening? He wasn't missing Helen too much?'

Helen was Carton Digby's wife.

'Are you trying to pick a quarrel, Giles?'

'Why should I quarrel with you, dear? You're perfect in most respects. And now I know how religious you are I'm certain you're virtuous.'

She did not answer.

'Yes,' he said. 'Rumour has it that you've spent five thousand pounds of our money – two thousand five hundred of mine, shall we say? – on a Christian cross. You must be religious to have spent most of our available capital all of a sudden, so confidently and high-handedly, and without consulting me. It must have been a bit like a death-bed conversion. Was the rumour false by any chance? Did you behave better than I think you did?'

'Oh Giles, spare me your sarcasm!' she railed at him.

'That's a dusty answer to a man who's two and a half grand poorer after drinking a couple of Cokes.'

'Religion's not why I bought the cross.'

'Why then?'

'Because we can afford it, and I'm not a miser, like you. Besides, Carton thought it could be very valuable, and he's an expert.'

'Are you in love with him?'

'Of course I am. Everybody is. He's a charmer. Any objections?'

'Certainly not. The object of my marriage to you was for us both to be happy ever after. And I'm delighted to be five thousand pounds poorer than I was a couple of hours ago.'

'We'll see, won't we, who's right and who's wrong about money? I'm not going to grovel yet.'

'And I'm not going to be beastly to you. I shall be my usual long-suffering self. However, just in case you've bought a pup, who did you buy it from?'

'Mikey Solomon.'

'Oh well! Let me have your receipt some time.'

'Shut up, Giles. You know there's no receipt. I forgot to ask for one. Stop bullying me!'

'We'll need the receipt, Melissa.'

'All right!' she screamed.

Giles Proctor was fifty, Melissa claimed to be ten years younger than he was. They had been married for twelve years; and now the basis of their marriage seemed to be a mixture of money or lack of it and discomfort.

He was thirty-eight when they met, handsome, eccentric, detached in all senses, more or less moneyed. At twenty-eight she was at a loose end and hard up. She had run out of married men, out of the bosses whose 'secretary' she had been, and was sick of sex on the trot, as somebody had described her brief affairs, sick of being single and at risk.

They did not fall in love. They fell for misunderstandings of each other. Giles saw in a pretty, healthy girl a chance that she would introduce him into a world he had never known, the world of the majority, of normality, of bourgeois values and contentment. She saw in an odd and funny man a promise of perennial surprises and amusement, with security thrown in to boot. They were not complementary. They were two of the kind that make matrimony unpopular – they were bad pickers.

She tried to look up to him. She had limited intelligence, and was conventional under her racy exterior. She did what she thought wives were expected to do, and bowed before his seniority and private means. But she was disappointed that he was careful never to lead the way.

Courtship was okay. He liked her drive, she liked his contrariness. She was at first tickled by his cat and mouse games. When she first said to him, 'I love you,' he replied, 'Hard lines!' She invited him to share her bed, to which he answered, 'How wide is it?' He was elusive: she would complain after he had disappeared for a day or a week, 'Where have you been?... Why do you leave me dangling?... I don't know what you're up to,' and he would only tell her, 'Ignorance is bliss... Ask no questions and be told no lies... I've been to Erehwon which is nowhere back to front.' His proposal was a joke: one night, after they had made love, he inquired, 'What next, Melissa?' That she should have thought him matrimonial material attested to the old truism that girls are got by tickling them.

Giles was unemployed, they both were, at the time of their nuptials. He admitted to being in need of remunerative work – playtime with jobs in second-rate schools or in the present-wrapping backrooms of big stores was over, while her savings had dribbled down the drain. They agreed to become shopkeepers, and went into the cheaper antique jewellery business as partners, living in the two upper floors of the house in Chipping Sodbury.

And there the pigeons came home to roost. Giles would not be pushed in any recognisably common-sense direction by Melissa, and she lost patience with his detachment. He took refuge in ironic mockery or sarcasm, and she was reduced to tears by, raged at, lost confidence in, and considered him less and less. They had their bones of contention: sex, money, the purchasing policy of Baubles and Beads, social life, all the major issues, in fact.

He was a disobliging bedfellow, and she believed he was deliberately ready and unready when she was the opposite. He was completely secretive about money – he paid the housekeeping bills precisely, shared with her the profit made by the shop, but only gave her more for hairdressers, clothes and suchlike under pressure. He was a stingy buyer at auction sales, she was open-handed – and her purchases were apt to be more profitable than his. He was reclusive, she was sociable – and so the arguments began, and never ended.

She often thought about adultery. Perhaps

it would rouse Giles's interest in his wife, perhaps it would serve him right. But she was reluctant to put herself in the wrong, and lose what was better than nothing. She had her special friend, Piers de Bray, who posed no threat to her marriage. He was a kind old bachelor, he sympathised with her sufferings, and in his elegant flat in the finest house in Chipping there was always his shoulder to cry on. Perhaps, on second or third thoughts, it was better for her to be safe than even sorrier than she already was.

Carton Digby was the stereotype of the men who irresistibly tempt women of Melissa's type in Melissa's position. Toweringly tall, broad-shouldered and straight-backed, with aquiline features, a ruddy complexion and intrusive pale blue eyes, oozing arrogance and wealth, he was much too much for her. The deadliest of the weapons in his seductive armoury was the common knowledge that he was bored by his mousey wife, misleadingly called Helen, and he was not above seeking consolation in arms less stringy than hers.

Carton had been a thorn in Melissa's flesh for years, ever since she set eyes on him. And he had compounded his offence by murmuring in an undertone as he shook her hand for the first time: 'You have a beautiful figure.' Frankly, she had always been impatient to show him more of it.

The episode in the Sheep and Goats carried things farther than they had gone before. Three days after it, Melissa met Carton by chance, by one of those coincidences the naughtier gods like to arrange, in the High Street.

He said to her, 'I was hoping to meet you,' she said to him, 'Same here.'

He asked: 'Can I have another look at that trinket of yours?'

She replied: 'Giles is minding the shop.'

He studied his watch.

'Would you be able to come to my warehouse in three quarters of an hour? It's over there, behind the bookshop. You'll see number ten on the door.'

'Yes.'

She did the rest of her shopping on legs that scarcely supported her and dumped it in her kitchen. She mounted the stairs to the matrimonial bedroom and picked up the cross that lay on her bedside table. She was racked by indecision. Giles had not been altogether wide of the mark: she had had religious inclinations once upon a time. But puberty was not exactly good for her, she became a promiscuous young woman, and morals were not the strong suit of her middle age.

But she was extraordinarily strong as well as weak. Her wilfulness reasserted itself. She was not going to let a little thing like adultery, or infidelity, or whatever it was that people with satisfactory husbands expected her not to do, spoil her sport and deny her a consolation prize. Her only concession to morality was that she did not take the cross to the warehouse, nor did she take precautions – she was unable to have a baby owing to the indiscretions of her youth.

The warehouse was suspiciously convenient, and the same applied to a sixteenth century *chaise longue* in a sort of arena surrounded by stacks of furniture. Melissa did not mind. She was grateful for the conveniences, and gave her all to Carton Digby twice in the space of half an hour.

Later, at lunch, Giles did not comment on her prolonged absence during the morning.

Over supper in the kitchen, however, he remarked: 'I admire the brightness of your eyes, Melissa.'

She blushed and was confused.

'Why are you blushing, my dear?' he asked with his customary lack of tact or mercy.

'You never pay me compliments,' she said.

'Oh – was it a compliment? I meant it to be an observation. Your eyes are unusually shiny.'

She guessed that he had probably jumped to the correct conclusion, but was past caring.

Carton was masterful. He was also impulsive and reckless in his private life, although notoriously canny in trade. He and Melissa became lovers without debating the reason why. More half-hours in the warehouse were exclusively action-packed. But in time they justified themselves, or tried to, by reference to their marriages.

Carton spewed his resentment of Helen, who, apparently, had insisted on separate bedrooms ten years ago – he was forty-five at the time and she was forty-one.

'She loathed sex – she shouldn't have married me, and I should have run for my life when she was stand-offish before we tied the knot... What the hell did she think I would do in my spare time at the age I was, twiddle my thumbs?... She blames me for womanising, and I blame her for not knowing men... And what use to me is a good mother of our children?... She's no helpmeet, she's a luxury I can't afford... I'll be giving her marching orders as soon as ever I can.'

Melissa's counterpoint ran thus: 'I don't know Giles any better now than I did twelve years ago, when he badgered me to marry him. I used to think him comical and supportive, but there are no laughs any more and we can't agree about anything. He won't – he loves to disagree – disagreement's about the only thing he does love. I don't know how much longer I can put up with our horrid life together.'

Carton's passion was not only physical. He swamped Melissa, or at least swept her off her feet, with his tidal waves of emotion. They fulfilled each other – each embodied the dream or one of the dreams of the other. They said they were happily in love; more accurately, they were relieved by their union, by the relief of their sexual communing which was nothing to do with Helen or Giles. They were both flattered, he by her adoration of himself, she by her conquest of this wonderful man whom every other woman in the world would welcome with open arms if they could.

It was not a big step from the point reached after a month or so to entertainment of the ideas of cohabitation and permanent residence within their own pleasure grounds. Divorce was an alarming word; but the plan of how they might shed their encumbrances and escape, and where they might live freely and lovingly thereafter, was exciting. Carton had enough money to oil all the wheels, Helen could be provided for, and his two sons had almost reached the age of reason and would probably be glad not to have to listen to their parents' squabbling. Melissa had no money of her own, but would not hesitate to exploit the crazy laws of the land and take the half of Giles' possessions that would be her entitlement.

Difficulties like ninepins were knocked over in turn. Carton made everything sound easy. Carton was a sort of Lord of Creation in Melissa's eyes – he created a new heaven and a new earth for her. The only fly in the ointment was the whisper into her ear that her prospects might be too good to be true. It reminded her of the cross she had bought and not yet attempted to sell. She had scrupled not to 'involve' it in her adultery: superstitiously she feared it might not approve. That Carton was inclined to describe their acts of love as 'showing the cross' grated on her nerves – she laughed, but unwillingly, and wondered how to bring her only criticism of his behaviour to his notice. Once, after their plans were near to becoming a project, she hurried home and in her bedroom held the cross in her hand, as if in expectation of receiving a message from it.

Soon afterwards, Carton burned a boat. In the warehouse he greeted her with the news that he had asked Helen for a divorce.

'Oh Carton! What did she say?'

'Not a lot. She doesn't believe me. But she will. Are you going to ask Giles?'

'Yes.'

'You know I want to marry you more than I've ever wanted anything.'

'Do you really?'

'I swear it.'

'Thank you, Carton. I'm absolutely honoured.'

'Will you marry me, Melissa?'

'Of course, of course I will!'

'Talk to Giles.'

She meant to. She tried to. But for a fortnight she funked it. She kept on apologising to Carton and making more promises. At last she summoned up the courage as they sat in their kitchen after supper.

'Giles, I want a divorce. Sorry, but I can't beat about the bush.'

'Do you now?'

'I'm serious.'

'It's a serious matter – and so sudden, dear.'

'Please don't make jokes – for God's sake, no more jokes.'

'Is Carton Digby the lucky or unlucky man?'

'What? What do you know about Carton Digby?'

'Two little things, if you're interested.'

'Go ahead!'

'You've been committing adultery with Carton, and he's not trustworthy.'

'I resent that. You're not in a position to call anyone untrustworthy – I trusted you, and look where it's landed me.'

'I'm afraid I don't follow you, but sorry if I've failed to please.'

'Oh Giles! I know you're not a bad man,

but you're bad for a woman. You're just not interested. You haven't made love to me for a year.'

'Not for want of trying.'

'Oh – well – no. I couldn't – it was too late. It's too late, Giles. You've mocked me for twelve years, you've undermined me and my confidence, and I'm not standing for any more.'

'How much do you love him?'

'He's the love of my life.'

'That does put the kibosh on us.'

'Oh – I do hate the things you say – but I'm sorry – I'm the sorry one – I still must have a divorce.'

'No problem – I mean I shall raise no objections – I believe there are things called irreconcilable differences, or something like that.'

She began to cry against her will.

'What have I done wrong this time?' he inquired mildly.

'I'm crying because you've made me happy.'

'For a change.'

'Please, don't make it harder than it is. What will you do, Giles? What about the shop?'

'It'll be goodbye to all that, I expect.'

'Are you unhappy?'

'Should I be?'

'There you go again! I'm going to talk to

a solicitor.'

'An unfortunate necessity if a divorce is required.'

'And I've no money.'

'Ah!'

'I'll have to ask for some.'

'No doubt.'

'You're richer than me, you won't be bankrupted.'

'Thanks for the kind thought.'

'Giles...'

She paused. He seemed not to be listening, he had never listened to her.

She continued: 'I've said my say. I think I'll go to bed.'

'That's a clever wheeze. Is the bed in the spare room made up? I'll sleep there tonight. Good night, my dear Melissa.'

She was more than ever confused by Giles, compared with whom Carton was transparency and simplicity. She was cross with herself for delaying her announcement – now Carton was attending an Antiques Fair in Berlin, he had been forced to take Helen with him, and then he was involved in a skiing holiday with his family for ten days. It was almost impossible for her to speak to him, and quite impossible for him to speak to her – they had regretfully agreed not to try to communicate; but if only she had spoken to Giles when she was told to do so, she would have had Carton on hand to congratulate and support her.

As it was, Melissa had not made a fuss about his holiday with his wife because he intended to break the news that he was actually in the process of suing for divorce. With luck, by the time the lovers were reunited, two unhappy marriages would be dissolved in all but legal detail, solicitors would be engaged, and obstacles between themselves and the promised land would only remain in place temporarily – that was their aim.

Accordingly, Melissa fixed an urgent appointment with Robin Eames at Eames and Westwell, Solicitors. She knew Robin personally and was impressed by his professional reputation. He was in his sixties, sympathetic in a dignified way. He undertook to talk to the solicitors used by Giles, Metcalf, Robinson and Phillips, and promised to do his best for her and obtain a decent settlement. He would write in a day or two, setting out schedules and prospects, and informing her of his firm's fees.

Melissa would have been more pleased to have progressed so far, if, at home, she had not found Giles preparing to motor up to stay with his parents in Scarborough.

She asked: 'Do you have to go immediately?'

'Do I detect a change of heart?' he replied.

'I thought you were in a hurry to be rid of me. Surely my people are entitled to know how I've been treated?'

'But what happens to the shop?'

'It's in your soft little hands. If you want to play truant, you could use our "Back in five minutes" sign, or else put up another saying "Closed for divorce and in hopes of living happily ever after".'

'Not funny, Giles. I'll have no transport if you take the car.'

'Carton Digby's got cars coming out of his ears.'

'Why are you so bitter? You never appreciated me – I can't believe my absence will make an iota of difference to you. Anyway, I've been with Robin Eames and he's going to contact Metcalf, Robinson and Phillips.'

'We are braced to repel boarders.'

'What are you talking about? When will you be back, Giles?'

'Oh no, my dear, you've lost the right to ask me such a question. Wait and see!'

He repeated 'Wait and see!' and laughed at her instead of kissing her goodbye as he drove off.

Her distress was reinforced by these exchanges; but so was her anger against Giles, who, thankfully, was soon to be only her first husband.

The next morning, Robin Eames provided

a possible explanation of Giles' advice and laughter.

Robin apologised for ringing rather than writing, but said he had urgent business to draw to her attention.

He continued: 'Philip Metcalf has informed me that Giles has virtually no money or other resources.'

Melissa denied it: 'That can't be true.'

'Apparently he told Philip he was penniless, and to pass on the message to yourself.' She tried to interrupt but he had more to say. 'Giles makes over to you the stock in the shop and the furnishings of your home. I wonder if you'll understand the other thing he wanted you to know, that he was not reclaiming the cross he paid for.'

'He owns our house – our house must be worth a fortune – what about that?'

'It's rented premises – the lease is running out – it has no capital value. I'm sorry to be the bearer of bad news, Melissa.'

'He's diddled me, you know. He's hidden his money. How can he have done it to me?'

'I suspect Philip Metcalf shares your opinion, although he couldn't say so. It's easy to spirit money away nowadays. I'm afraid I have a question for you to answer. Am I to go ahead with proceedings for your divorce?'

'My God, yes – and urgently! Goodbye.'

She rang off. She was too agitated to be

polite. She needed Carton Digby. She was at a loss, then decided to have it all out with Giles and rang his parents' telephone number.

His mother answered.

After brisk preliminaries, Melissa asked to speak to Giles.

'He's not here,' his mother said.

'Honestly?'

'What do you mean, Melissa?'

'You're not fibbing for Giles's sake?'

'Fibbing? I don't tell fibs. I'm sorry, Melissa, but I don't think you should talk to me as you have.'

'Sorry, sorry,' she said, and again rang off.

At that moment, before she could work out where Giles was and what he was doing to her, the doorbell rang. It was a letter from Carton, delivered by one of those private postal firms. Her spirits soared above recent tribulations and tiresomeness – her lover had made part of her wish come true by post – he had said he might write and been as good as his word.

She opened the letter and read: 'Darling, I can't divorce Helen, I cannot say the word, I'm too kind or cowardly. Please please understand. Please please forgive me. Please please please can we go on as we were – always, for ever – please? Your loving C.'

She was by her front door, in the hallway of the house that belonged to some unknown landlord, and she sank on to the floor. She surprised herself by not crying – there was no remedy in tears. Three, she thought – disasters come in threes – she had had to do to Giles what Carton could not do to Helen, she had found out that she was on the breadline, and she had been worse than jilted, she had been persuaded to ruin herself by a man who betrayed her in order to have his cake and eat it. Her hero was a cad. Her husband was a better bet than her lover. She had made mistakes. She had behaved badly. She was being punished for her sins.

Later in the day she was able to drag herself round to Piers de Bray's flat. He did not fail her. He was unlike the other men she had loved in every respect. He listened to her, he gave her food and drink, mostly drink, and insisted on her sleeping in his spare room.

She stayed with him open-endedly, and they sorted out her future between them. She only left Piers' flat late at night because she was fearful of meeting Carton. She guessed that he knew where she was and despised him all over again for not having the nerve or the decency to try harder to contact her. No, she told Piers, she would not oblige Carton's selfishness, she never wanted to see him again; and she was too ashamed of her treatment of Giles to seek him out and beg for reconciliation. And no, eternally grateful to Piers as she was and would be, she could not be his consort or his wife. She would move on, leave Chipping Sodbury, look for a job as far away as possible from the scenes of her downfall. Her mother was still alive – she would try to be a better daughter than she had been.

Piers helped Melissa not only to reach these decisions; he rendered assistance over her cross, the jewelled one, first by rationalising her mystical attributions of her sorrows to it, secondly by involving himself in its disposal.

She had never pretended to Giles that she had bought the cross for God's sake, although it might have saved trouble. It might even have lulled Giles into not guessing that she had spent his money in order to purchase the attention of Carton Digby. After it was hers, dormant memories of her Christian upbringing stirred. The cross seemed to be a blessing. She was happier with it than without. She had recollected one of the Commandments: its contrary effect on her was like a love potion. She was temperamentally inclined to do what she was told not to do; and knowing in her bones that Giles did not deserve to be set aside, and that she should not lead on or be led by Carton, was an irresistible incentive to sin. She now saw herself as the casualty of vengeance from on high, from some superior judge whose instrument and agency was her little cross. Impossible, unreasonable, primitive, foolish, Piers assured her repeatedly.

Well then, she explained, she wished to find a good home for that scrap of metal and its jewels, as if it had been an unwanted puppy or an abused child. She needed money and to sell it to the right person, who might benefit from possessing it – she would not sell it at auction. At last Piers mentioned Aaron Colquhoun, a friend of his who was ill, a rich man who lived in a fine house, The Grange in Old Sodbury, an awkward customer, also a scholar, antiquarian and philanthropist, who Melissa knew by name.

Piers went to see Aaron Colquhoun. He reported back to Melissa that Aaron was prepared to buy the cross for two thousand five hundred pounds, half the price she was asking for it and no more. He did not like it much, he had said he was too old and ill to go on collecting things, and that its power to interfere in human destiny was balderdash, but, considering the sad circumstances of its owner, he was prepared to make his offer. Piers added that Aaron had looked like a dying duck, and she ought to make up her mind quickly.

She sold it. She believed Aaron needed it, and she needed his money. She left Piers, she left Gloucestershire, and in time regained her equilibrium. She did not marry again, despite having chances.

A Worshipper of no God

Part of Old Sodbury was down in the Sodbury Vale and part climbed up the hill towards the plateau above. Aaron Colquhoun's house was situated on a sort of shelf on the hillside. It could hardly be said to belong to the village since it stood in a couple of acres and was flanked by farmland. Its name, The Grange, had been chosen by Aaron because it was the opposite of any recognisable building with agricultural connections.

The man who lived there, and had designed it, had it built, and thrown it in the face of the people he was pleased to call 'the sods of Sodbury', was now in his seventies, unwell, yet still inclined to affront and offend. Aaron Colquhoun was born rich, and had complained for half a century of being 'bled white' by taxation. He was a mixed bag of strong qualities and defects, a ladies' man of yore who was irritated by women, a charmer with a gift for putting backs up, a wit who could be humourless, a mean benefactor, an idler and a scholar, a conventional contrarian, considered by various persons either wise or mad. Perhaps the unifying factor of his personality was his addiction to trading.

Now, at his age and in his state of health, he resembled a shrunken sharp-beaked bird probably of the crow family. His eyes behind his spectacles retained the malicious glitter of a magpie's. In the old days he must have been bigger and stronger, although always short of stature; and no doubt would have had the arrogant bearing of most men who have realised how rich, clever and virile they are. That his money was new was not an aid to niceness: he was the indulged only son of a self-made Scottish millionaire, who had done him the additional favour of dying young.

Aaron sold the industrial assets he inherited, and settled down to being a dilettante: which contradictory description is typical of his story. He won women's hearts or bent them to his will. He besieged and battled with them, and lost interest when they could fight no longer. He collected things obsessively, and then sold one collection or another and began again. He mugged up more knowledge of antiquities than is known by the majority of antique dealers, and took pleasure in telling them that the etching or the corroded bronze bowl he had just bought for fifty pounds was worth five hundred. He gained a reputation as one of the cognoscenti of the arts, and was appointed by inane politicians to serve on quangos that were meant to unearth and subsidise genius: he disrupted their meetings and brought them into disrepute. His interest in the arts was peculiar to himself: he recognised early on that they were the ideal means by which to annoy and mock his fellows. He bought bad pictures as well as good ones in order to make fools of his friends, and punish the people who thought they could cash in on his perspicacity.

He really was a bastard in the popular usage of the word, euphemistically he was a maverick, and to those with steely nerves and stomachs to match he was amusingly different, something else, an individual who did not give a damn, a good old British eccentric.

The Grange was the eccentricity of his latter days. In an extended village of cottages and houses built of wood or bricks or the grey stone quarried near Chipping Sodbury, he erected a mansion of concrete and glass in the Walter Gropius *Bauhaus* style. It was angular, it was painted white, and Aaron would allow no greenery to grow on it. That it was admired by architectural buffs, that it was admirable in relation to respectable criteria and even historic in a minor sense, mollified none of the locals – which might have been part of the object of the exercise.

Aaron was never averse to showing people round his house. His comments were designed to make them grind their teeth, which were already set on edge by the wide open spaces and whiter than white walls of the interior.

'I need a picture window here so that I can see my ships sailing into Bristol loaded to the gunwales with African slaves,' he would say. He was more than politically incorrect, he was a political *provocateur*. When his visitors were duly provoked, he would inform them: 'But my great African friend, Professor Botlawyo, made the joke about slaves – I thought it funny – I thought it as funny as he did – I'm sorry you – or should I say "we"? – are not amused.'

Alternatively he would confide in strangers: 'I'm an exhibitionist, I like to switch on all the lights in the house at night and copulate with my wife in full view of our neighbours. Poor sods, why shouldn't they share our fun?'

Then he would apologise to a clearly unlovable and unloved wife or a withered spinster: 'I beg your pardon, my dear, for failing to spot that fornication was unlikely to be your line of country.'

He had married twice. He had had mistresses galore – and not only when young; but it was more convenient for him to combine the posts of housekeeper and butt of his humour in one person who lived in and was in constant attendance. His first wife, Miriam, a gentle Jewish girl, had not lasted long: that is she bolted, or rather fled, soon after she had borne his son – and with reason and extra haste when he insisted on calling the boy Adolf, after Hitler. His second and present wife was Barbara, whose departure might have been postponed on account of his illness.

He had cancer and was not expected to keep going for long. His changed prospects brought about no transformation of sinner into saint, or even an improvement of his manners and behaviour. Intellectually he grew more dogmatic and offensive, rammed his atheism down any handy throat, blasphemed without mercy, asserted that the gulags were a figment of Solzhenitsyn's imagination, denied the Holocaust, and preached the urgent necessity of the final solution of the problem of international liberalism. Moreover his teasing acquired a sharper edge – Barbara lost her daily ladies who were not prepared to be addressed as 'Skullion' and 'Skivvy'. But, at the same time, his secretive virtues were accentuated along with his vices.

The miser could be generous. The cruel husband, the harsh master, was sometimes kind. Now Barbara caught him leaving twenty pound notes in cooking pots and dustpans for the staff. A stranger arrived, a youth, to thank Aaron for money that would give him time to write a book on some abstruse subject. He and Adolf had quarrelled, needless to say, but Aaron wished to see his grandson, a boy of twelve; and when, in consideration of his health, that wish was granted, he concealed his cloven hoof, charmed and encouraged Jack, and they became close enough friends to irritate Jack's father.

Aaron's purchase of the cross from Melissa Proctor was another example of the magnification of his mixed motives. He shelled out two thousand five hundred pounds for it because of old acquisitive habits, because he had money to burn, because he knew the cross was worth more than he was paying, and because it inspired him with an idea for his swan song, more accurately his final blast on the trumpet of his destructive doctrines. But, also, he liked Piers de Bray, Melissa's middleman, he was pleased to do Piers a favour, he revelled for a change in the role of benefactor, and he said he was sorry for the girl – he said he pitied all the sex-crazed half-witted masochistic girls, who cannot wait to take it lying down from men such as he himself had been.

Barbara Colquhoun was twenty years younger than Aaron. She had been another of the casualties of adultery when they met

– cheated by her long-term lover, who had decided to be faithful to his wife, past child-bearing age, fighting a lonely battle with her regrets, and seeing no pleasurable future ahead. She was not much to look at, and her intelligence drew the line at any fool in a pair of trousers.

Aaron was different. He was more different than she knew at first. He was dashing, vigorous, and had a weird extravagant sense of humour she could laugh at. His impatience was complimentary – she was happier than she had been for ages not to keep him waiting. And his proposal struck her as more honest than extraordinary.

He had rung the doorbell of her flat at seven o'clock in the morning and said to her when admitted: 'I want to marry you, but I'm here to beg you to turn me down. I'm a monster, make no mistake about it, and don't think for a minute you'd be able to reform me. If you say yes, I'll do my damnedest to ruin your life. Oh, you'll be comfortable and so on – nothing else – no comfort from me is on offer. Why am I telling you this tripe? You'd suit me, and I suppose there's an outside chance that you could bear me better than some. Incidentally, I wouldn't leave you high and dry, I'm too old to change partners again, often again – and that's not a threat, although you may think it is.'

Her reply was not affirmative, but she laughed at him and let him into her bedroom, which was roughly the equivalent of yes.

Unexpectedly, even against her own private expectations, Aaron's single positive opinion proved not to be erroneous. Barbara seemed to be capable of withstanding the worst of his blasts against her and the rest of the world. She was one of those lucky people whose looks benefit from the passage of time. In her later forties and thereafter her complexion changed from good to better, her face gained a welcoming homeliness, her smile was excellent – ever-ready, teeth strong and white – and her hair turned naturally from mouse to a pretty grey-blonde. Meanwhile her torso spread sufficiently to become a buffer capable of absorbing the shocks and tribulations of a monster's wife. Eating was an unfailing consolation, and her additions of flesh insulated her nerves.

Aaron and Barbara rubbed along together either gratingly, emitting sparks and flames, or with comparative and compensatory smoothness.

His ill-health was almost less of a surprise than his gladiatorial health had been – he had asked for it with his anger and cigarettes. Of course, it altered none of his ways obviously. He continued to smoke and to rail against everything and nothing. Barbara had to admire his courage and stoicism; while her feeling for his other attractive qualities, and her recognition of his Quixotic tilt against the windmill of his height, his battle to be big somehow or other, were reinforced by his attempt to be debonair in the valley of the shadow of death.

But his purchase of the cross turned the screw of tension at The Grange. Religion had been a bone of contention between the Colquhouns, since Barbara was a Christian and a believer of the non-churchgoing kind – it would have driven Aaron madder than ever if she had gone to a Communion Service at St John the Baptist's in Chipping Sodbury. For a moment, after Piers de Bray's visit, when Aaron dangled the jewelled object in front of her face, she wondered unrealistically if he had thought better of his atheism. Then, as hope was ousted by experience, she jumped to gloomier conclusions, that he had bought it partly to play games, that he was about to behave worse than usual, and the cancer must be getting more of a hold over him.

Their first exchanges on the subject of the cross were ominous.

He said to her: 'Don't run away with the idea that I bought it for you, my dear, to encourage your weak-mindedness, or out of the goodness of my heart.'

She retorted: 'Why do you have to pretend

you're nastier than you are? I think it's silly. Piers was grateful to you for helping that poor woman.'

'Piers is a sloppy old fool.'

'That's not true. He's clever, and he's your friend.'

'Listen to me, Barbara! I bought the blasted object, which isn't a cross in fact, although you've chosen to think it is, to make money. You're always after my money for housekeeping – well, I'm going to make it to shut your mouth. But before I sell and rake in my shekels, your "cross" must serve my purposes, as you'll discover before too long.'

'What purposes, Aaron? Don't frighten me.'

'Patience, my dear.'

'Oh, I don't know how you dare to be such a devil in your state of health. Why can't you be nice?'

'Because I was born not to be the nice sort of bore who wouldn't have kept you on your toes for so long.'

On another occasion she asked him: 'What is the cross if it isn't a cross?'

'I'm giving a lecture about it shortly.'

'What? You're not fit to lecture anyone, Aaron.'

'I'm fit to call the bluff of idiots.'

'But how? A lecture where? And when?'

'In this house – I'm having the invitations printed.'

'Who are you inviting?'

'Neighbours – people who love me – not a large gathering.'

'But you've always hated gatherings of all kinds, and you've never been hospitable. Are you serious?'

'The answer to your question depends on how seriously you regard religion. Personally, I think religion is a hoax, and expect our guests to greet my lecture with gusts of laughter.'

'Oh no. You're not intending to poke fun at religion?'

'I intend to shed light on it.'

'Don't, Aaron, please! It's wicked to try to destroy people's faith in God. It's not funny, it's not clever, it's not worthy of you – please don't.'

'Well, I'm afraid for once I must disappoint you, Barbara.'

She desisted, she knew it was a mistake to argue with him, but in a day or two, at a propitious time, she spoke her mind again.

'Aaron, I'm afraid you've forgotten what other people are like, and it does sadden me that you have no sympathy with them in their illnesses and sorrows, and no pity. It was one thing to nag me about religion, but it will be another to broadcast your views and rob harmless strangers of their faith and trust in God, in any of the gods, and their hope of life after death.'

'Too bad,' he replied.

She persisted: 'My other worry is that your lecture will be the death of you.'

'If so, good riddance – that's my opinion – over and out!'

In due course the invitations arrived, and her help was required to send them to the fifty persons on Aaron's list. The wording of the invitation caused Barbara further concern, it was so boastful and blasphemous, and ran as follows: 'You are invited to hear the last words of the famous scholar and antiquarian Aaron Colquhoun on a popular subject – *God, is He dog spelt backwards?*'

Potential guests were told to arrive promptly at six-thirty p.m. on such and such an evening, warned that late-comers would not be admitted, and promised champagne.

She dreaded it. She foresaw catastrophe. At the same time, oddly, that is typically, it came to her notice not that Aaron was slipping downhill faster than ever owing to the strain and excitement of organising his lecture, but that his disease seemed to be in remission, and he himself to be stronger and more energetic than he had been for months.

Only ten people turned up. Barbara received them, and she and her daily lady served the champagne. Aaron waited offstage, and, when she reported to him at six-thirty as commanded, he summed up his audience as three bleeding hearts who had come along to be in on his death throes, three liberals who did not know the difference between good and bad, a downtrodden woman married to a barrack-room lawyer, and a couple of Christians bent on forgiving him. He gave orders not to open the front door again, and with Barbara in tow marched into his drawing-room and, to very muted applause, sat on a stool behind a small table and faced his audience, scattered amongst the superfluity of chairs. He sipped water from the glass on the table – Barbara seated herself in the back row – and in his sharp clipped manner, now without much volume, he spoke.

'Welcome to my home.

'My first name, Aaron, is unusual. I was not baptised, my father was never a Christian. He called me Aaron for three reasons, to keep within the law of the land and register my birth, because its origins are connected with mountaineering and taking risks, and thirdly because he had a soft spot for the brother of Moses, the Aaron who set up the golden calf for people to worship while Moses was receiving the Commandments from Jehovah.

'As a result, I must warn you that I am a risk-taker and a heretic and urge you to leave the room if you are easily shocked.'

A titter or two filled an uneasy pause.

He reached for the cross that lay on the table, held it up, and resumed: 'I bought this a short time ago. My Christian wife believes it to be a Christian cross, and for all I know you may be disposed to agree with her. Mistake number one: it is a cross only in secular terms – two pieces of metal welded at right angles to each other. For Christians, whether or not they know it, the cross is a crucifix.

'Crucifixes are representations of the crucifixion of Jesus Christ, you are tempted to inform me. Where's the body, you would like to ask. Mistake number two: in the early days of the Christian Church, graven or pictorial images of the son of God were taboo. Crucifixes were required for religionists to worship, but, by pious respect or commercial pressure, they had to leave more to the imagination than became fashionable in less godly ages.

'Look again at the object I hold in my hand. I have not yet dated it, I have not had time to consult metallurgists or the carbon brigade. But I – or you – could suggest it is a typical example of the solution arrived at by the artisans who supplied the demand for crucifixes a couple of millennia ago. The semi-precious stones, cut or filed into the cabochon shape, and set into the metal, masquerade as the figure of Christ. The green peridot at the bottom of the upright represents feet, the purple amethyst above it the torso, and the rose beryl and the citrine the right arm, and the blue topaz and the garnet the left arm.

'What a pity the hole at the top of the upright is not filled, you think. What a shame it's gone west! Mistake number three: although I myself could be mistaken, and you could be right to think one stone is missing, I have to tell you that often our superstitious forefathers were unwilling to create or possess any approximate mimicry of the most sacred of all the sacred parts of the anatomy of their Saviour. And I would suggest that the hole is blank on purpose.

'Now, if you will, note that the stones, plus the setting for the stone that is not there, amount to seven. Numbers have been lucky or unlucky since the dawn of time, and luck and religion are closely related. We have been considering the possibility that I bought a crucifix, a Christian artefact, but the number seven was sacred in the ritual of the Hebrews, the Jewish people of long before Christ. We hear of seven altars built, seven sacred wells, seven lamps, blood being sprinkled seven times. We know the seven day week, and should have an inkling that a Jubilee is seven times seven years and occurs in a fiftieth year: Jubilee equals Hebrew "Yovel".

'Seven reaches farther back and into countries other than Palestine – Babylon, Sumeria, Egypt, India. Their objects of worship include the seven planets, seven planetary deities, seven heavens; and theirs was the physiology that perceived the seven substances and seven natures of man.

'Look once more at this so-called cross or so-called crucifix! You could not crucify a grown man on a cross with the proportions of this one – a dwarf maybe, not the Christ of the New Testament. The upright is too short, the crosspiece too long. Indeed, I may be doing dwarfs an injustice by wondering if they would fit proportionally on a cross that seems to be made for an orang-utan.

'The conclusion I have reached, the probability my qualifications have arrived at, is therefore that the thing I have been showing you is a con trick. The metal is metal and the jewels are not glass, but the rest is a booby trap. It looks a bit like a Christian cross but is the wrong shape, imitates a Christian pattern but uses Hebrew symbols, and with its seven stones would have us believe that it hails from the ancient world of primitive idolatry and preposterous creeds. Far from being a holy icon, it is a fraud and a catch-all fake.

'Why then did I buy it? Fakes are not always worthless, as the trade in archaic Chinese bronzes proves. But, although I was tempted by avarice to acquire this fake at a knockdown price, I have realised that I shall need money no longer in weeks or days. I therefore have an uncommercial agenda in connection with the cross, and have summoned you this evening to hear the summing-up of my lifelong investigation of the relationship of the Christians' God and His children, as they like to think of themselves. Humanity grows old, too old for fairy stories. Religions testify to nothing but the feebleness of our race, which refuses to recognise truths that stare it in the face. Gods did not create us, we created them with our wishful thinking. Nature does not care whether we live, die, suffer, flourish, and God, whoever He is or claims to be, is certainly subservient to nature. Death is a full stop. The only form of resurrection and the afterlife is whatever grows from earth we have fertilised with our blood and bones. Christianity is one of many...'

Aaron hesitated. His sharp nose looked sharper in his white and deeply lined countenance. Barbara stood up, fearing he was going to be ill or worse.

He started the sentence again.

'Christianity is... Christianity is for...'

He could not finish it. His eyes behind his glasses showed white, his head sank forwards, he began to slip off the stool, banging his head on a corner of the little table and upsetting the cross and his glass and jug of water on to the floor, and collapsed into the arms of Barbara, who had rushed forward. A member of the audience, one of the more muscular 'bleeding hearts', provided assistance. The daily lady was summoned, and Aaron was half-carried out of the room.

The other members of the audience exchanged glances, grimaces, remarks in an undertone, and the barrack-room lawyer sniggered – their reactions to the dramatic conclusion to Aaron Colquhoun's lecture and perhaps his life, and to the possibly divine intervention which had robbed him of the chance to cast further aspersions on Christianity.

They filed out of the house tactfully and almost on tiptoe in the absence of their host and hostess, the Christians amongst them trying not to look smug.

Aaron survived. He revived. A week passed, and then a fortnight. All was roughly as it had been before he gave his lecture. But there were two differences, which surprised Barbara. The first was that he began to eat more than he had for months; and she suspected, despite medical prognoses, that he was putting on weight. Secondly, he departed from his egoistic practice and never boasted about or even referred to his lesson on atheism.

Surprise was not Barbara's only response to these developments. She was afraid he must have had a stroke or some other type of seizure, which had affected his memory and might be the beginning of Alzheimer's Disease. And she was ashamed to acknowledge that, having adjusted to the ideas of her difficult marriage coming to an end and of her future of widowhood and freedom, she dreaded a prospect of looking after Aaron, Aaron incapacitated and even more of a pain in the neck on a permanent basis.

But she was a good sort, and submitted herself to the will of her God, who was apparently not incensed by Aaron's pinpricks.

In the third week after the lecture the Colquhouns kept their appointment with Aaron's cancer specialist in Bristol, Professor Campbell. Various tests filled the morning, and the Professor interpreted them in the afternoon. He was happy to report an extraordinary improvement – the progress of the cancer had been arrested, tumours had shrunk, the patient was more robust, and he could not explain why but hoped his treatment would continue to have beneficial effects.

They returned to The Grange. Another week passed, still with Aaron in his uncharacteristically dreamy state, but now looking better for all to see. It was Barbara who certainly felt, and no doubt looked, worse – she could foresee nothing but trouble, and felt sure that her husband was again up to his tricks.

One afternoon, when she had thought he was asleep in his chair in the sitting room, he demanded: 'Where's my cross?'

She answered question with question: 'What did you say?' She was angry – it was as if he had pressed the button that at last made her blood boil.

'My cross, my cross, where is it?'

'What cross?' she retorted. 'You told us the cross wasn't a cross, it wasn't even a crucifix, it wasn't Christian, it was nothing important or worthwhile, and I expect it got thrown out with the rubbish.'

'What's bothering you, my dear? You seem excited. Are you unwell?'

'Yes, I am, I'm sick, sick of you. I begged you not to make that stupid speech – no, Aaron, it wasn't clever, it was just insolence – but you took no notice, you would do it in your pigheaded way, and I hated it, every horrid little word of it, and now our neighbours cut me in the supermarket and are more than ever convinced that I'm married to a lunatic.'

'Calm yourself, Barbara–'

'You're not to talk to me like that, not any more. I've kept calm when I thought you were on your last legs, and let you order me about and never say thanks, but you're well enough to treat me properly, politely anyway, and better than you have treated me for all the years I've been your wife and your slave.'

'It distresses me—'

She interrupted him again.

'Don't talk to me about your distress – you have no right to be distressed – that right's mine. And I won't be patronised and patted on the head, Aaron. Take care, I'm warning you – if you have a relapse you'll expect me to nurse you and be kind, kinder than you've been to me.'

'My apologies, Barbara. I must plead for your patience for a little longer. But I would like to correct your impression – my contention was not that the subject of my lecture was rubbish.'

'Really? Well, you fooled me. You made fools of the people who came to listen to you.'

'My dear, it might be a mistake for the pot to call the kettle black, but I do believe my lecture went over your head – you can be obtuse at times, if not exactly stupid.'

'And you can always be depended on to be rude.'

'Thank you. You see, I have thanked you. And I'm sorry we happen to have bone-headed neighbours. But, to cut short this conversation which has deteriorated so far as to be worthy of fish-wives, may I remind you that I merely asked if you knew the whereabouts of what you would like to think is a holy relic.'

'Don't mock, Aaron.'

'It isn't mockery to try to expose lies and the snake-oil salesmanship of crooked priests and shamans, and to hit ignorance on the head with the truth.'

'Oh Aaron, you're as ignorant as you consider we all are. Your mind is closed to whatever you don't happen to know. You mock your cross, you sneer at your cross. Why do you think your cancer's cured?'

He opened his mouth to answer back, but did not speak and did not close it. His mouth hung open, and he gazed into her eyes as he had not for years, perhaps inquiringly.

She put her hand on his shoulder and asked: Are you all right?'

He now closed his eyes and whispered rather pathetically: 'Leave me, dearest.'

She obeyed yet again. She stood up and took a moment to decide to say: 'Aaron... The truth... The truth is what I've told you,' and went and found the cross amongst papers on the desk in his study.

She was not summoned to return to the sitting-room. Her eventual offer of tea was refused with a wave of his skeletal hand. She waited, was pleased to hear him totter to the lavatory, was undecided, and at six-thirty strode in and spoke to him.

'What do you want for supper, Aaron?'

'Nothing,' he replied.

'You must eat, you had no tea. Would you like an omelette with salad?'

'Nothing,' he said.

'What's wrong?'

'My life is ruined.'

'Nonsense – you're on the mend.'

'No – no more – I cannot live with your idea that I'm on the receiving end of a miracle.'

'How do you explain the recovery you've been making? Professor Campbell couldn't explain it, he just took the credit.'

'I've denied lots of things I shouldn't have denied. In the end I was only convinced I was right to deny the hocus-pocus of religion. Intellect has been everything to me, and I can't accept that my intellect led me astray.'

'Poor Aaron!'

'You could be wrong, too.'

'Yes. But Piers de Bray thought the cross might help you to cope with your illness.'

'He didn't say so to me.'

'Can you wonder at that? You would have sent him off with a flea in his ear.'

'I'm finished, you know.'

'Stop it, Aaron! Why not trust the cross or the power that's in the cross to continue its good work?'

'No cowardly conversion at the eleventh

hour – I've laughed at them too often.'

'What about the omelette?'

'Women are so physical! Very well. The ideologies of men are turned into fiascos by women. Give me a hand upstairs, if you'll deign to mix your cruelty with mercy.'

'Thank God, that's better!'

'Speak for yourself,' he said.

She escorted him to his dressing-room, where he had preferred to sleep since he fell ill although they had always had twin beds in the matrimonial bedroom. She made him comfortable, and fetched and served his supper. Later, she supervised his pills and ran through the routine of preparing him for the night.

He spoke to her gently, almost sweetly, with a worrying touch of pathos.

'You haven't answered my question.'

'What question?'

'The one that has had such unfortunate consequences.'

'Oh that! The cross is downstairs. Shall I get it for you?'

'If you like. If you will.'

She did so and laid it on the bedside table.

She said: 'I'm sorry I upset you earlier. I can't tell whether or not it's the cross that's done you good. Nobody knows such things.'

'But you believe, don't you, that an object of a certain shape and substance can be imbued with omnipotence?'

'Oh Aaron! I'd put it another way. We don't know everything, no one does.'

'I feel guilty.'

'What?'

'It's too late to change my spots.'

'They say it's never too late.'

'Dear Barbara, my life has been devoted to picking holes in what "they" say.'

'You'll feel more like yourself in the morning.'

'Yes, yes. Thank you again. At least you know for certain now that I'm grateful.'

'Aaron...' She was more worried. 'Shall I leave you? Will you be all right?'

'Quite all right, whatever that may mean. Good night, my dear.'

'Ring if you need me. Good night.'

She left him. He never rang. He had died peacefully, as they say. His bedclothes were not disturbed.

Youth's Priorities

Barbara Colquhoun did not know what to make of Aaron's death. She had expected and yet was shocked by it, because it was so sudden. She was not sorry: personally, privately, she felt as if she had shed, or had been relieved of, an intolerable burden. On the other hand, had she been partly responsible for his death? Had she at least hastened it? And what were the influences brought to bear on recent events by the crucifix – the Sodbury Crucifix, so-called by Aaron.

Admittedly she had spoken to him sharply on the day before he died; but she was under pressure of accumulated anxiety at the time. She had not meant to be unkind, and her reproaches were surely mild and definitely overdue, for she had suffered his lecture in silence. She had not complained before of the trouble in the neighbourhood it had stirred up, and she had not taken noticeable umbrage because he had ignored her pleas and wishes. All she had done was to put forward one of many interpretations of the phenomenon of his conquest of cancer.

It was contrary of him to over-react to her

135

tidings, which would have been considered glad by most men and a reference to a signal honour; and his reaction was no excuse because it was characteristic. His career had been devoted to arguing that black was white – if he was clever he was too clever by half – it had been idiotically obstinate of him to maintain that the homicidal mania of Communism in power and the Holocaust never happened – he should have gained enough experience and humility in a long life to realise he could be wrong, and accept that religion might be an elucidation of certain mysteries. He had talked of science, of evidence, of the absence of proof of the power of the Almighty; but his explanation of the creation of the universe was no more convincing than the one in the Old Testament. He had sought the limelight, to be singled out from the masses – how perverse, in that case, to die of having been told his life was saved by means beyond the ken or the reach of the mass of mankind.

Barbara was no more logical than her husband had actually been. Lack of logic in different contexts was probably one of the unrecognised bonds between them. She struggled against her guilt by telling herself that she had expressed an opinion, no more, and he had taken it unreasonably hard. Women with common sense see more clearly than men with a weakness for 'ideas'.

She knew in her bones that she was only guilty of minor misdemeanours, and was reinforced in her belief that the opinion she had aired was not absurd.

For what had Aaron not just been nearly resurrected by, but also died of?

She found him lying on his back with the cross in his hands. She had removed it before the arrival of Dr Wood, who diagnosed immediately that Aaron had died of cardiac failure. In time she received a letter of condolence from Professor Campbell: he wrote that Aaron's sudden death had been predictable, even though not directly caused by his cancer. There was either no Coroner's Inquest, or Barbara was spared it by those who had taken charge of her husband's remains. She did not challenge the medical version of his death – she had had a surfeit of denials; but nor did she rule out the possibility that her God had seen fit to forgive Aaron's heresy and grant his ultimately negative wish.

The complexity and difficulties of faith were not a problem. Barbara's common sense included the recognition that Aaron was right to have called her an ignoramus. She did not know if Christianity was everything it claimed to be – and the same applied to other religions – but so what? She was a Christian, she loved her religion, and took in her stride the references to the

Virgin Birth and the Trinity.

Anyway, now, she was faced with practicalities more pressing than metaphysics. She had Adolf, her stepson, who had changed his Christian name by deed poll to Dolf, and Dolf's son, Jack, staying in her house. Dolf was in his fifties, looked rather like his father, beaky, on the short side, and had a similar awkward temperament, but held views that were the exact opposite of Aaron's. He was a Roman Catholic convert, had christened his son and written letters to newspapers disassociating himself from his father's views; in return for which his father had kept him as short of money as innumerable rows and threats of legal action had allowed. Dolf was a professional librarian in London, and had come down to Old Sodbury to see about his father's will and no doubt what was in it for him, and to discuss the funeral with his stepmother.

The first difficulty, apart from Dolf's aggravating manner and manners, was that no will was to be found. The consequence was, the assumption was, that Barbara was therefore the sole beneficiary of Aaron's estate. Dolf did follow in the paternal footsteps to the extent of denying it. He began to turn The Grange upside down in his search for the will, while dropping hints that he would have to sue for the lion's share of the spoils.

Meanwhile he congratulated Barbara for aiming to give Aaron a Christian burial, but objected to her not wanting to bury him locally, where his militant atheism had made enemies. She said that the rectors of the Sodbury churches might well refuse to do the job, and that she dreaded to be charged with hypocrisy. Dolf accused her of having weak knees, and favoured a family show of disagreement with all that Aaron had stood for.

A lot of the unpleasantness that had re-entered the house was caused by Dolf's treatment of Jack. He bullied his twelve-year-old boy in just the way he had repeatedly accused his father of bullying him. He sneered and jeered at Jack, and drew attention to the blushes he himself had summoned. His mercenary frustration was Jack's misfortune.

Barbara winced at the interrogations that began early and finished late: 'Why are you late for breakfast?... How do you propose to help your father today?... Are you to be trusted to clean your teeth, or would you like me to have a bash?'

The abuse was incessant when Jack was instructed to search cupboards and drawers. 'You clot!... You'll pay the price if you don't find the bloody will – you'll get no more free lunches... Why are you so cack-handed?... Do it properly, for pity's sake!'

Jack had inherited the looks of his mother, a pretty blonde called Heather who had run away from Dolf to marry a more amiable man. He was condemned by legalities to spend half his free time with his father in a London flat and the other half with his mother at his stepfather's cottage in North Berwick. Barbara rescued Jack when she could, telling Dolf that she needed help with shopping.

Towards the end of Jack's stay she asked him about his school.

'What's it called?'

'Crabtree College.'

'Where is it?'

'In Yorkshire.'

'It's a boarding school, isn't it?'

'Yeah.'

She tried again.

'What do you do in London?'

'Not much.'

'I mean, when your father's at work?'

'Nothing much.'

'What's it like in North Berwick? Do you enjoy yourself there?'

'It's cold.'

But after two or three such abortive conversations she was both startled and pleased when Jack asked her: 'Was Grandpa evil?'

'No,' she replied. 'No – he had a rebellious spirit – do you know what I mean?'

'Not really.'

'He couldn't accept things as they were or as they had been for ages.'

'Father hated him.'

'They were too similar to get on together.'

'He didn't believe in God, did he?'

'No – no for most of the time – but he thought he was doing good in his own way.'

'Father says he didn't go to church.'

'That's true. Do you go to church, Jack?'

'Yeah, too often.'

The visit of Dolf and Jack ended better than had seemed likely to begin with. Barbara promised to hand over the major part of Aaron's wealth, including The Grange, as soon as her solicitors had prepared the requisite information and paperwork. As a result Dolf was gracious enough to say that he could not care less what became of his father's corpse.

On the morning of their departure Jack looked so glum that Barbara asked him in an aside: 'Would you like to come and stay with me for a few days on your own in the summer holidays?'

'Yeah – thanks – I really would,' he replied.

'Well, I'll talk to your father.'

Barbara organised a very private funeral for Aaron in the church at Didmarton, for his cremation afterwards, then scattered his ashes at night in the herbaceous border of The Grange garden, hoeing them in so that her part-time gardener would not notice.

The solicitors delayed, strange to relate. Barbara remained in Aaron's 'white elephant' – the nominal tit-for-tat of his neighbours for whom he had rude names. She already had an understanding with an old friend in Chipping Sodbury, who wished to move into an eventide home; but she could not buy her friend's house or tie up any loose ends while she waited.

In due course she obtained Dolf's permission to have Jack to stay – Dolf was relieved to think he would not be saddled with his son for at least some of the time they were authorised to be together.

Barbara met Jack's train at Temple Meads Station in Bristol. The boy did not look well. He was pale and thin, and had no trace of the summer tan she had expected him to have acquired on cricket pitches and playing fields. He was quiet even in comparison with the monosyllables of his previous visit, and showed no excitement to be back in the land of the Sodburys.

Barbara sighed. She was afraid that he was a chip off the fatherly and grandfatherly block after all. He communicated his tension to her, some straining of his nerves, some disharmony in his soul, which was sadly reminiscent of her married days. She would have to work hard to regain lost ground, that is the confidence in her that he had tentatively demonstrated with his acceptance of her invitation.

At The Grange he was not easy to entertain. He seemed to be short of concentration. They conversed by means of question and answer sessions.

'When did your holidays start?'

'Three weeks ago.'

'Were you pleased to finish with school for a bit?'

'Yeah.'

'Your school's in Yorkshire, isn't it?'

'It's a college.'

'Sorry! Are you happy at Crabtree College?'

'Okay.'

'I'm very pleased to see you again, Jack.'

No answer.

'Would you like to see your grandfather's treasures?'

'I don't mind.'

She led the way to the study, he slouched behind. She produced photographs of family groups, of Aaron holding forth at Speakers' Corner, of Aaron with Oswald Mosley and on a picket line at Nuremberg. She obtained a flicker of interest when she handed him the pellet shot from an airgun by one of Aaron's hecklers and extracted by a surgeon from his lower back.

Food was less of a failure than other topics.

'I've got sausages and mash for supper...
It's roast chicken and chips for lunch... Ice
cream with chocolate sauce... St Clement's
Cake...'

'Lovely, Aunt Barbara... Thanks!'

She drove him to the movies in Bath, to
Wookey Hole, to a fairground in Yate; but he
was not rewarding, he almost merited his
father's jibe that he was lackadaisical.

By the end of the second day of his visit
she was sure there was something wrong,
and her questions became more personal.

'Are you feeling quite well, Jack?'

'I'm fine.'

'Is anything worrying you?'

'No.'

'Can you keep up with the work at
school?'

'Yeah – it's easy.'

'Too easy? Are you bored there?'

'No.'

'You seem not to be yourself, if may say so.
Could I help?'

'No, thanks, Aunt Barbara – I'm all right,
honestly.'

She ventured to probe into his relations
with his father.

'I imagine Dolf's bark is worse than his
bite, because of his likeness to Aaron, an
awful barker. Is that true, Jack?'

'I don't know.'

'I mean, is he kind to you?'

'Oh yeah.'

'Was it horrid for you when your parents divorced?'

'Not really. Most of the parents of the boys at Crabtree are divorced.'

'You're closer to your mother than to your father, I expect?'

'He hasn't got much time.'

'Time for you?'

'Well, time for anything, except work.'

'When did your mother last see you?'

'In the Easter holidays, before Grandpa died.'

'That was months ago.'

'She's pregnant.'

'Oh – is she? – that must make a difference – but does she speak to you on the telephone?'

'Yeah, sometimes.'

'Would you tell her if there ever was anything wrong?'

'Nothing's wrong.'

'Anyway, you'll have lots of school friends. Are you a member of a gang?'

'No – I'm a loner.'

'But a happy loner, I hope?'

'Yeah.'

Her final attempt to break through his defences or guarded privacy was also repulsed.

'Jack, do you sleep in a dormitory at your College?'

'Yeah.'

'With boys of your own age?'

'Some older boys.'

'How old are they?'

'Seventeen about.'

'How many boys sleep in your dormitory?'

'Twenty.'

'Do you sleep well?'

'Okay – I'm okay, Aunt – don't worry.'

Barbara herself knew insomnia only vicariously, because Aaron had suffered from it, especially when stressed. She had imagined that Jack might have inherited his grandfather's trait, and, despite getting nowhere with her line of inquiry, she wondered if she had touched a spot sensitive for some reason. That was no doubt why, in the night that followed, Jack's last night in her home, she was woken and immediately wide awake.

The unusual sound she heard was a regular moan. The time was eleven-thirty. She hoped at first that a wind had blown up and into the chimneys; but her window was open and the air outside was still. Her second thought was that a burglar had broken in and injured himself, cut an artery on broken glass and was bleeding to death. The moan was regular, like breathing, distressed breathing. She got out of bed and cautiously opened the bedroom door. The sound issued from the spare room in which Jack slept.

She had been frightened, now she was

concerned. He was having a terrible nightmare, and she did not know what to do. She stood indecisively on the upstairs landing, where a light was left on at night, and hoped he would wake of his own accord before she went along the passage and knocked on his door.

After a moment she overcame her shyness, she could not let him moan more and more miserably, and moved in the direction of his room, whereupon his door opened.

She was startled in the extreme – the automatic cry of his name stuck in her throat – she saw that his eyes were half-closed and showed only the whites – realised he was sleepwalking and remembered having been told that sleepwalkers should be woken gently or not at all.

He walked towards her and into the landing as if he could see, slowly but without hesitation, not feeling his way, continuing to moan with his mouth contorted. It was uncanny, and her heart thumped with either sympathy or horror. But she was afraid he would try to descend the stairs or fall down them, and moved involuntarily to stop him. He bumped against her, into her, his eyes opened, he yawned, recognised. his surroundings, saw her, emitted a noise between an ululation and a lamentation, and began to cry and shed huge tears.

Barbara was not sure if Jack was fully awake during the talk that ensued between his bouts of violent crying.

She had embraced him in her warm strong arms and led him back to his bedroom, where she switched on the lights and they sat together on the side of his rumpled bed.

'Poor Jack, poor Jack,' she repeated, patting and stroking him.

At length she had a chance to say, 'You've been having a nightmare.'

'I was at school,' he sobbed.

'What was happening to you, Jack?'

'Billot and Mudie were there.'

'What? Who are they?'

'Bad boys, seniors, bad...'

'Their names are Bullot and Mudie?'

'Billot.'

'What do they do?'

'They say things, then laugh at me, they make the others laugh.'

'Why? Are they teasing you? Are they making jokes about you?'

'I don't know.'

'What things do they say?'

'"Come behind the pavilion... Tuck me up in bed... Wash me in the showers."'

'Oh dear!'

'What do they want? I haven't done anything wrong.'

'You don't understand?'

'No, no... Why am I so unpopular?'

'It isn't that, you poor boy. You mustn't think that – I'm sure you're popular with your friends. They haven't... These two seniors, they haven't ragged you? They haven't touched you, Jack?'

'They just say things and laugh.'

'No physical contact?'

'I hate school.'

'Let me wipe your tears away. You'll be all right now. I'll see to it that you are. Get into bed and go back to sleep. Sleep peacefully, Jack. Don't worry any more.'

He did as she told him. He slept as soon as his head was on the pillow. She left the light on and the door open and returned to her own bedroom, leaving that door open too. Jack did not stir for the rest of the night – Barbara was sure of it since she paced about, listening, or sat in a chair, thinking and waiting for the dawn and the next day.

At breakfast, when he wandered down to breakfast, she asked him: 'How are you?'

'Fine, thanks.'

'Oh good! I've cooked you an egg and bacon, which should sustain you until you get to London.'

'Thanks.'

'You had a nasty dream last night.'

'Did I?'

'Jack, you eat up, I'm doing toast for you. You're leaving me today – I'll miss you.'

'So'll I.'

'The Grange will soon be your home – it'll belong to your father – and I'll be living in Chipping Sodbury. Will you come and see me there? Don't answer that question! But remember I'd love to see you.'

'My autumn term starts next week.'

'I know.' She hesitated before asking, 'Do you get away from school – at half-term, for instance?'

'We have three weekends out.'

'How long is an outing?'

'Thursday till Sunday.'

'You'll be home again quite soon.'

'I suppose so.'

'How's the egg?'

'Fine!'

'Do you remember your dream? I hope you don't, it was a nightmare.'

'I don't think I do.'

'You were so sweet, you fell asleep again after you'd been upset. You had a little sleepwalk. Do you go sleepwalking often?'

'Sometimes.'

'It must be tricky in your dormitory at school.'

'Yeah.'

'There's butter and marmalade and honey – take your pick – and here's the toast.'

'Thanks, Aunt Barbara.'

'You told me things last night – about school – the things that upset you in your nightmare.'

'What things?'

About Billot and Mudie.'

Jack blushed and stopped eating, and Barbara was worried he would start to cry.

She added hurriedly: 'I'm so glad you told me, I'm honoured that you confided in me. Do those boys really pester you?'

'Sometimes.'

'They were bad in your nightmare. Are they as bad as that in real life?'

'I don't know, I don't understand them.'

'Oh Jack, you will – you'll grow up and understand – they're funny with you because you're young and good-looking – it's nothing to do with unpopularity.'

'Don't tell my father, please, Aunt – please don't tell him.'

'I give you my solemn promise that I won't. There! But have you thought of complaining to the headmaster?'

'Oh no, I couldn't, I can't – you won't tell anyone, anybody, will you?'

'I've given you my promise and I keep my promises always. Are you thinking of taking any steps to improve your situation?'

'No – I can't – it's not on.'

'Well, I'm thinking of something that might help.' She picked up her bag, rummaged in it and produced the crucifix. 'Are you religious, Jack?'

'I have to go to a Catholic church at school.'

'That's not what I meant – but it doesn't matter. You see this cross? Yes, well, it might be a Christian cross, or, according to your grandfather, it might be a crucifix, the Sodbury Crucifix, or else, in his not very reliable opinion, it might be just a lucky charm dating back to the year dot in the Middle East. Do you know what a crucifix is?'

'Sort of.'

'It represents Jesus on the cross. Apparently these stones, plus the missing stone at the top, are meant to be the body of Jesus. But your grandfather told us all that in one breath, and in the next said none of it was true – he was such a maverick. All I know is that he liked the crucifix enough to buy it, and it brought him good luck once or maybe twice. And personally I believe it's a bit more than lucky. And I'm thinking of giving it to you.'

'Golly!'

'It's valuable for every reason.'

'Gosh!'

'If you took it to school with you, and treated it carefully, it could repay you with much better luck than you've been having.'

'But it's yours, Aunt.'

'Exactly. I inherited it from your grandfather. I inherited everything, but your father's entitled to most of it, which is only right and proper. I don't want any arguments, particularly an argument over the

Sodbury Crucifix. The point is that I'll keep your secret, and you must keep mine – that I consider the crucifix my own and that I'm at liberty to give it to you. Do we have a deal?'

'I promise never to tell Father.'

'Thank you. Now, there's one other condition attached to the gift. In your first short holiday from school, when you're living in The Grange, or even if you're still in London, will you please let me know if the crucifix has made any difference? Will you make that promise too?'

'I will. Oh, Aunt!'

She held it out to him, and he stood up, knocking back the chair he had sat on, and hugged her, as he never had before.

She laughed, embraced him, put the crucifix in his hand, and, to keep emotion to a minimum, suggested that he should finish his breakfast.

Barbara got over the death of Aaron quicker than outsiders expected. She was not slow to realise that it was silly, if not hypocritical, to pretend to miss someone who had made her life as difficult as he could, whatever his mixed motives and however pitiable he might have been. She was grateful for the compliment of his proposal of marriage, and for interesting her with the peculiarities of his character and intelligence; but the reliefs of widowhood were that her thoughts were her own, and money likewise. She felt happy every morning instead of apprehensive, and she gained confidence with every passing day.

Dolf, of course, was a trial; yet he served a useful purpose in reminding her that Aaron was no longer going to aggravate her as his son did. The solicitors and accountants, and at length the Inland Revenue, were able to provide sufficient information for her to decide how much of the estate she wished to keep, about one fifth, and how much she would be prepared to offer Dolf. He disagreed. He spent money he could ill afford on having her figures checked by his solicitor and accountant. He niggled about a picture, a standard lamp, a rug, a lawnmower. He was unfriendly, hostile, unapologetic, pitiful, his own worst enemy, like Aaron.

She was practised at dealing with the type, and eventually her treatment of carrot and stick had the desired effect. Dolf had been so preoccupied by mercenary matters that only after the settlement was complete he remembered the remains of his sire and benefactor, and asked what had become of them.

Barbara told him, and he raised pained eyebrows at the mention of the Protestant funeral at Didmarton and a groan of Catholic horror in response to the cremation and the disposal of the ashes.

He opined: 'I can't say I approve, Barbara.'

She returned: 'You certainly can't, Dolf, you have no right to express any view, since you behaved towards your father alive and dead in a thoroughly un-Christian manner.'

They parted on polite terms nonetheless. She apologised as well as quelling him, for the sake of Jack she was careful not to burn boats; and Dolf – to deny him the benefit of the doubt – would not have forgotten that Barbara was childless and might return her fifth of the Colquhoun estate to the family coffers.

She moved out of The Grange and into 14 Horseshoe Lane in Chipping Sodbury. She was more excited than regretful; and when all the agitation of the last weeks and months had subsided, and her personal responsibilities were whittled down to near zero, she had time to concentrate on the plight of Jack and to hoping he was getting on better at Crabtree College. The question that preoccupied her was whether or not he would keep his promise to give her the good or bad news during the first of his three outings.

He did. Not long after she was installed in Horseshoe Lane, on a Friday morning, he knocked on her door. He had changed as much as children of his age can change in a short space of time. He was taller and his voice was beginning to break. In respect of his bearing, complexion, facial expressions and manners, he was a different boy. He was all smiles and liveliness.

'Hullo, Aunt Barbara! How are you?' He accompanied his greeting with an uninvited kiss on the cheek. 'Have you got a minute? Can I come in?'

His visit was brief, but long enough. He seemed to fill her sitting-room with sunshine. He said he was sticking to their agreement, he had wanted to because she had been so kind to him when he stayed at The Grange. He added that he had other plans, to meet friends who, he had discovered, lived in the neighbourhood, and to do some bicycling.

'Have you been happier at school?' she asked.

'Oh yes – it's not so bad this term.'

'Are the two boys pestering you still?'

'Which boys?'

'Billot and Mudie.'

'Oh, them! Billot got sacked for work and Mudie's in another dormitory.'

'I'm so glad, Jack.'

'What's it like down in Chipping, Aunt?'

'I love it.'

'Are you sad not to be in The Grange?'

'No. Do you like it there?'

'I do, so does Father.'

'The cross seems to have done the trick.'

'Oh, yeah.'

'You've still got it, Jack?'

'Yeah.'

'Do you think it has odd powers, or are you as sceptical as your grandfather was – perhaps as he was only until the last hours of his life?'

'I don't know. You believe it's magic, don't you?'

'No one knows anything, that's my opinion.' They laughed, and she continued: 'But I have some faith in it, yes. Where are you off to now, Jack? Don't let me stop you.'

'I'm going to buy sweets and things.'

'I remember your sweet tooth.'

'Goodbye, Aunt – see you!'

But Jack did not see Barbara during his second outing. She scarcely expected it, assumed he was spending this one with his mother up north, and pinned a hope or two to the third, reserved for his father, the date of which she had obtained from Dolf.

Most of the weekend in question passed without a sign of Jack. On the Saturday morning, in her natural way, without hesitation, she rang The Grange, spoke to him and, undeterred by his man's voice and unenthusiastic tone, invited him to call.

He accepted. He was late. She opened the door to a stranger, another inch taller and covered in spots. His looks were ruined by acne, he was probably shy for that reason, and did not compensate for his appearance by announcing at once that he was in a hurry.

'I wanted to know how you are,' Barbara explained.

'Okay.'

'And school, Jack?'

'Okay.'

'That's all. You run along.'

'Sorry, Aunt.'

'Why? You've got your life to lead and I've got mine. Thanks for letting me get a glimpse of you.'

'Sorry all the same.'

'What do you mean?'

'I've kept away.'

'I don't understand. There's nothing to be sorry for.'

'I lost the cross.'

'Oh.'

'Yeah.'

'Oh well – we all lose things – it can't be helped. Did it happen at school?'

'Yeah.'

'When?'

'After the first outing.'

'How did you lose it?'

'I swapped it.'

'Swapped it!'

'I was afraid to tell you.'

'What did you swap it for?'

'A box of fudge.'

'Oh no!'

'Peters – he's a friend of mine – his father gets fudge from a special shop somewhere – and I suppose it was wrong.'

'Yes. Was the fudge good?'

'Okay.'

'Let's change the subject. Do you have exams this term?'

'We've had them.'

'Did you do well?'

'No – failed.'

'What does your father say?'

'That I'm good for nothing.'

'Do you mind?'

'No.'

'Do you mind anything now, Jack?'

'Not really.'

'Well, goodbye and good luck.'

'Bye, Aunt.'

After he had slouched off she realised that her faith in the cross was reinforced.

Too Late – the Rabbit's on the Plate!

The five Sodburys of Gloucestershire were not unique in England: they all had, and may still have, their share of snobs. The snobbery of location, which exerts such a strong effect on the prices of property, ranged from top to bottom in the following order: Chipping, on the Hill, Little, Old and Lower. Yet each Sodbury could claim an advantage over the others. Thus Chipping Sodbury could consider itself the biggest and best, Sodbury on the Hill was superior geographically and because of its long views. Little had an aristocratic manor and was discreetly hidden on its hillside, Old was nearly as good as Chipping and was thought by some to be Chipping's smart suburb, while Lower had the distinction of being raffish and unbuttoned, despite its popular little church that looked like a farm building.

It would be hard to single out one snob who was more snobbish than the other snobs in the Sodburys – again, the area was like the rest of England. But Sir Eugene Peters was thought by many to deserve that prize to add to his KCB. He lived in Sodbury on the Hill. He had bought a good

Cotswold stone house called 18 Sodbury Drive, renamed it Peters Place, replaced boundary fences with walls and installed electronic gates in his driveway: that was twenty years ago. He was a retired Civil Servant – he preferred to say he had worked in central government – and looked and behaved more like a not particularly civil master. In his mid-seventies he was still a tall handsome man with strong features and a good head of white hair. His arrogance was obvious, although he put on a show of old-world courtesy, and his dignity came in for mockery in some of the Sodbury taverns.

His career was not noteworthy. He had idled his way to the goal of his knighthood. His finances were secure, and his hobby and the pastime of his older age was his collection of somewhat banal curios. The drama of his life was his relations with women. He was, he liked to think he was, he clung to the idea that he was or had been, a Don Juan.

He had married and divorced twice. His third wife, Milly, was much younger than he was, but too old to bear his only child, his son and heir – she died of the effort. As a widower, he had summoned his former secretary and mistress, Mona Welby, to console him. She was his everything, but he would not marry her – he was one of those men who do not respect the women who

162

sleep with them out of wedlock.

Matrimony and cohabitation were by no means the whole story of his love-life. He was born with an insatiable appetite for female flesh, he hunted and gathered the opposite sex, adultery might have been his middle name, and his testosterone had no conscience. His appearance was not to every woman's taste: he was too big, too like a barber's block, too impatient, boring, unsubtle and untrustworthy. But he could be more appealing than his female rejects and other men knew, gentler, more flexible, and his blitzkriegs and persistence often succeeded where charm failed.

Boldness and courage redeemed some of his other characteristics. The animal trainer who puts his head in the lion's mouth nightly and twice on Saturdays serves as a metaphor descriptive of his sexual exploits. He needed all his courage when his sexual prowess puttered to a stop. He was humbled. He was mortified. He confided in no one and made excuses. He hinted that he was having medical treatment in the relevant region. He removed himself from Mona's bed to the bed in his dressing-room. He let her know by his usage of the past tense and absence of action that he had either gone off her or was again in the process of changing partners.

Extra strain was incurred by the arrival of

Mrs Macdougal in Chipping Sodbury. She had bought a cottage at the top of the High Street hill, in a side street there, and was soon invited to all the social gatherings of the local bigwigs. She was a divorcee, a pretty little brunette with a melting manner and a ready laugh; and although she presented a dire threat to wives and even more so to female partners, she was decorative, put the men in a good temper, minded her ps and qs, and was essential fare at every successful do.

Eugene Peters pined for her. She looked half his age, although gossip said she was years older; but at first sight the regretful thought crossed his mind that she might have been his last love. He immediately managed to get on to the terms of flirtatious badinage that would undoubtedly have led to the joys of sex in days gone by. He called her Gloria after talking to her for five minutes, while she refused to call him by his Christian name, she said she did not dare, and would address him as Sir Eugene, with the sweetest pretence of awe and admiration. They greeted each other at parties with sighs of mutual relief, indulged in conversations that seemed to him to be all wit and promise, and parted with wrinkled brows and signals of resignation. The tragedy for him was that he could not accept her invitations to drop in on her. He had to summon up his reserves of self-control not to stroke her and kiss her cheek as if he was kissing her lips, or make the slightest move that could land him in an embarrassing fiasco and perhaps ruin his reputation. He never went out socially unless Mona came too.

At home he consoled himself with his memories. He laid out his collections of cigarette cards, ashtrays for pipe-smokers with pipeholding attachments, seaside post-cards, historic cricket balls, and suchlike. And he salvaged some pride in recollecting the existence of his son.

His name, Eugene, stood for nobility, and he chose the unusual Christian name Ingram for his son because it means a raven, the greatest of the family of crows. He wanted Ingram to be strong and forceful, had tried to compensate for his motherless childhood, and sent him to Crabtree College because it taught religion, politics, business and survival skills, which should equip him for one way of the world or another. He was disappointed to discover that Ingram's chums at Crabtree called him Inky, and that the boy was overweight and the opposite of a high-flier at his lessons.

However, Eugene was gratified when Inky produced the Sodbury Crucifix.

'What's this?' he asked.

'It's a crucifix.'

'Who says so?'

'I got it from Colquhoun at school. His people live at Old Sodbury. His grandfather knows his stuff, and he said it was a crucifix.'

'That must have been Aaron Colquhoun. He's dead.'

'Well, he said it when he was alive.'

'He was a poseur, he was an anarchist, I don't take his word for anything. Are these stones real?'

'Yes, Dad.'

'I think they're glass.'

'Jack Colquhoun said they were half-precious.'

'What did you pay for it?'

'I didn't pay a penny.'

'A p, please.'

'Well, a p – sorry.'

'How did you get it then?'

'Swapped it.'

'For what?'

'Sorry, Dad, swapped it for the box of fudge you sent me.'

'This stone could be an amethyst.'

'Jack said it was.'

'How could anybody work out that it's a crucifix? There's no figure of Jesus Christ.'

'He's in the stones.'

'What about the hole?'

'It's Jesus' head according to Jack.'

'He must have been teasing you.'

'He wasn't, Dad, honestly.'

'If you're right you'll have pulled off an astounding deal. I congratulate you, Ingram. May I take charge of it and show it to one or two experts?'

'I want you to have it, Dad – you paid for the fudge, didn't you?'

'Funny boy! Thanks all the same. I'll buy you more fudge without delay.'

'Dad, Jack said...'

'Yes, what else did he say?'

'It's lucky, it's got lucky power or something.'

'Indeed?'

'Jack could have said that to make me give him the fudge.'

Mona Welby was an ex-victim. She had been the least favoured of her parents' children, unpopular with her siblings, treated badly by a succession of men, and had then fallen into the arms or the trap of Eugene Peters.

At the time she was a Civil Service secretary, a neat efficient blonde with a hard-boiled cynical outlook and a wry sense of humour. She was in her fortieth year, hoping to find a husband and have a child, but her new boss, Eugene, had other ideas, and she stood out against him for mere days. He was married at the time and made it clear that he would not divorce his second wife to make an honest woman of Mona.

Thus time passed and dashed her maternal hopes. And to make matters worse for her, he met a younger woman, Milly, and did divorce his wife, explaining to Mona that Milly could bear his child whereas she could not.

When Milly died after giving birth to Ingram, Eugene summoned Mona back to the fold – Peters Place – to be the consort of his declining years. She was twice shy. She struck a hard bargain. She would have no means of support or financial independence if she came to heel when he whistled: he would have to buy her companionship with a sizeable sum. The unexpected result was that for fifteen years she had not been unhappy.

First of all, she was fond of Eugene in an almost motherly way. She knew him through and through, and saw that he was a ladies' man in the sense that he belonged to the ladies. He was dependent on them and, to an extent, on her. Secondly, she would be well off in every sense if he either kicked her out, or the bucket. Thirdly, he could no longer hurt her feelings with his philandering – she had renounced jealousy. Last, and most importantly, she had become an owner and breeder of dachshunds of two types, and they fulfilled her spirit and occupied her busy days.

She was an OAP, and he had received the

state pension for years. His virility in the past had given her the key to a kind of secret sunny garden, where old wounds healed and humdrum worries were discarded along with her clothes, and she could live for love alone and the pleasures of the flesh. But, to pursue the metaphor, autumn had invaded her garden, and the paths of dalliance were increasingly overgrown by weeds and thorny tendrils. Sex tailed off. When Eugene remarked one dark night that she was freezing up and not giving him the necessary, and he would not trouble her further and intended to sleep in his dressing-room in future, she let him get away with it, she did not puncture his pride, although she had every reason to know the truth of the matter.

The exclusion of sex from their equation had side effects that suited her quite well. Her seductive clothing, threadbare as most of it was, was turned into dish-cloths and dogs' beds. Her daily attire consisted of trainers, corduroy trousers and a knee-length kennel coat, and in the evenings, after an occasional bath, she threw on a Jaeger dressing-gown that had belonged to her late mother. She did not cut her grey hair – she pinned it up when she remembered, and she bought spectacles in thick black frames. Her general appearance was the equivalent of the stuff called Keep Off, which she applied to her bitches that she wanted not to mate with any old unselected dogs.

She still lived *with* Eugene, but *for* her dachshunds, the two smooth-coated miniature bitches, Ruby and Sapphire, and wirehaired Beryl. She now could have them to sleep in her bedroom. She drove them to dog shows in distant locations partly to have a break from domesticity. She was up with her dachshunds in the morning, not the lark, and took them for walks, often along the bridleway that passed by Hetty's Pot on the Sodbury Holding farmland, and spent the rest of her time, when she was not cooking for Eugene or listening to his monologues, attending to, feeding and taking them to the vet. The nearest she ever came to her former interest in sensuality was her attendance at canine mating sessions, and the resultant litters of puppies which she looked upon as her grandchildren.

Imagine her surprise, therefore, when, shortly after Ingram's third autumn term outing from Crabtree College, she was disturbed in the middle of an afternoon by Eugene with a recognisable twinkle in his eye, demanding instant sex. She happened to be in the outhouse that she was allowed to use for the visitations of the suitors of her three little girls: an association of ideas might have brought her lover back to the boil. She wanted, but knew better than, to laugh at him. She felt ridiculous with her corduroys at half-mast. She obliged in the necessary hurry, and hoped for no repetition.

Unfortunately from her point of view if not from his, he returned to the charge. Another metaphor, borrowed from the French, had always applied to him: his appetite was sharpened by eating. He was uxorious again, and again in inconvenient places – he said he could not do it in her bedroom in front of her dogs at night. Perhaps she should not have been surprised by his readjustment of the clock: she reminded herself that he had been looking healthier and fitter than for a long time. Somehow he had recovered not quite his youth, but his middle age. She asked him what was going on, had he taken drugs, where had he got his second wind, and would it be too much for his strength? He answered everything in the negative with complacence.

It was nothing to do with the crucifix, he insisted to himself. He was not a religious man, except in so far as he felt it was the duty of the Establishment to support the Church of England. But he was too rooted in this world to believe in any other, or, for that matter, in any power greater than bureaucracy in general and the Civil Service in particular. He had smiled indulgently when Ingram repeated that old wives' tale about the 'luck' of the crucifix – he could immediately recall a score of scandals involving 'living saints' and 'miracle-working objects'. He was not gullible – he was above hocus-pocus.

He had boasted to Mona of Ingram's precocious acumen and shown her the crucifix. She sniffed at Ingram's robbery of Jack Colquhoun and was not otherwise interested – her gods and goddesses had four short hairy legs. Eugene rambled on about Aaron Colquhoun being wrong about most things, but Mona had not listened. He put the crucifix on his desk, preparatory to stuffing it in one of the cupboards where he kept his collections.

Yet he himself was aware of an improvement in his health, mental as well as physical. He was more energetic and optimistic. And day by day he notched up degrees of the revival of his confidence.

He expressed gratitude to Mona, for instance by offering to help with chores. He almost begged her for shopping lists which he would attend to in Chipping Sodbury. On his third or fourth shopping expedition he managed to run into Gloria Macdougal in Steve's, the greengrocery.

'Hullo!' he exclaimed.

'Sir Eugene!' she returned with equal enthusiasm.

They talked for a few minutes, he drove home in a happy frame of mind, and, in order to speak the adorable name of the woman, mentioned their meeting to Mona.

Mona looked at him, a rare occurrence these days, and he had the grace to feel he had been caught out.

He shopped more often for Mona. He lingered in Steve's for Gloria. He again ran into the latter in the less frequented part of the shop that sold exotic fruit and veg.

She said to him: 'What an admirable man you are, Sir Eugene, to stoop to women's work!'

He said: 'Shopping has its rewards.'

Her smile acknowledged the compliment, but she said: 'Your wife must be pleased with you.'

'I'm no longer married. Mona was my secretary for many years, and leads her own life with her dachshunds under my roof. I understand Mr Macdougal has fallen by the wayside.'

'He lives in Scotland – which I suppose comes to the same thing.'

She giggled at her joke.

He smiled and pursued his strategy.

'Do you approve of Chipping Sodbury?'

'I do. I love my little nest. Won't you drop in and let me show it to you?'

'Thank you very much.'

'For instance one morning after we've bought our greens?'

'For instance tomorrow?'

'Eleven o'clock, Sir Eugene, at number fourteen May Street.'

'Perfect! *Au revoir!*'

He had not exaggerated. Not only her face, figure, elegant trouser suit and hospitable offer had struck him as perfection, but he also felt at home with her, knew where he was in her company, for she spoke the language he had learnt in his amorous heydays, and had participated in the game of seductive double meanings.

He walked away from her with his head held high and shoulders back, he was again the dominant male, untroubled by doubt that he might prove not to be the cock of the walk; and twenty-four hours later he rang her doorbell.

He was again dazzled by her appearance – she was a member of a species utterly different from the female population of the Sodburys. For that matter there had been nothing like her in the Civil Service. She glowed. She was ageless. He could not wait to lay hands on her.

The sitting-room was tiny, seemed to be full of flounces and bows, reminded him of a boudoir, and smelt of lilies of the valley.

He admired it. She laughingly said he was too big for it. They sat side by side on a small sofa and drank cups of coffee. There were photographs in silver frames, mostly of

174

Gloria with a variety of men, skiing, sun-bathing on a yacht, in tweeds on a hillside.

She waved a well-manicured hand at them and said: 'My rogues gallery.'

'Who are the rogues?' he inquired.

'Husbands!' Her grimace was a mixture of displeasure and penitence. 'I've been a Butcher and a Stott – my first two husbands' surnames. The Christian name of the Macdougal of that ilk is Willy.' She laughed out loud. 'I have a chequered past, you see. And you, Sir Eugene, are now in my parlour.'

He repeated his request that she would drop the Sir.

'Not yet – all in good time.' It excited him to hear her promise them a future of some sort. 'What are your secrets, Sir, she said?'

They laughed together, and he boasted that he had suffered from having had an excess of women.

'Poor you!' She laughed at him – she was verbally tougher than expected. 'Are you a Bluebeard? The Bluebeard and the spider with a parlour, a fatal combination, don't you agree?'

He did not agree, but he refrained from disagreeing.

'What brought you to Chipping Sodbury of all places?' he asked.

'What brought you?' she retorted.

'Perhaps we were brought here to meet.'

'Sir Eugene, am I on your shopping list?'

'I wish you were, my dear Gloria.'

'Oh well, we'll have to see about that, won't we?'

They continued this conversation until their coffee cups had been empty for a quarter of an hour. She then stood up, ending the audience, and escorted him to her front door.

'I already hope to see you again,' he said.

'You shall – by arrangement – my phone number's in the book – is yours?'

He was not keen on her ringing him and speaking to Mona, but confirmed that it was, and kissed her on the cheek as well as shaking her outstretched hand.

At their next meeting she again said something he was not sure he liked. She said that she was still good friends with her three ex-husbands, and grateful to them after all, since between them they had set her up financially for the rest of her life. Was it a warning that she was a gold-digger, he wondered. On the other hand she had sanctioned a brief necking session on the sofa, and it inspired him to feel more reckless than he could remember ever feeling before.

His parting shot on that occasion was to refer to her claim that she was finished with matrimony, and add: 'But not love, Gloria, your kisses deny that you're finished with love – I refuse to listen to the word *finito* in

176

that context.'

She replied with a thrilling glance composed of thanks, shyness, frailty and titillating humour: 'I suppose I must begin to try to call you Eugene.'

At their third meeting they reached the stage at which people no longer young and ripened by experience cease to see the point of the conventions and the moral boundaries.

That nothing serious actually happened was due to several factors, to Gloria saying it was too early, and reminding Eugene of the fate of Uncle George and Aunty Mabel, and barring him from her bedroom because he was too big, and perhaps to Eugene not forcing the issue.

But he was keener than ever to have her, and sure he could please after practising with Mona. Plans that would brush aside her objections and feminine fancies formed and were reformed in his overheated mind. He imagined himself renting the Hawkesbury Monument for an afternoon or evening, and proving his consummation of their love affair in front of an audience of six counties. He was dismissive of London – he was too well-known there. And Bath was too close, and provincial into the bargain – and how was he to convince Mona that he was taking a holiday in England on his own?

Abroad beckoned – Paris would be ideal –

a weekend by Eurostar first class – a hotel with a name – the Chateaubriand in the first Arrondissement – how could she refuse?

She said two things he wished she had not said. She wanted to know the number of rooms at the Chateaubriand, and pulled a face when he told her only twenty-five. As for his suggestion of Thursday to Monday, she insisted on Wednesday to Sunday as the shops closed on Mondays. He had not counted on such hard bargaining – love was the goal, not showing off in a huge hotel or shopping. But her kisses mended fences. He deceived Mona, or decided to think he had, with his lies. He bought the tickets and made the reservations.

The evening before his departure he was tidying his desk and noticed the crucifix. A question occurred to him while he stowed away his passport, traveller's cheques, paper money etcetera. He answered it in the negative. His access of health and strength was attributable to nothing but his own fine constitution. And he had always had luck with women.

He opened one of his cupboards and tossed the crucifix, which he believed was simply a cross and probably jewellery, into an open box of items he had recently bought and intended either to include in his collection or to sell. It lay on top of antique toothpicks and slides for men's ties, and he shut and locked the cupboard door.

They travelled separately to London. He had not been there for several years and was flustered by the queues and traffic jams. Then she was late at Waterloo, and he was worried that he would meet some inquisitive acquaintance and again by her uninhibited laughter at his fears.

Eugene was so confused by Paris that Gloria had to take charge of getting them to the Chateaubriand Hotel. Unfortunately she was not too pleased by the room and bathroom she had insisted on having to herself, and Eugene was also displeased to find that the cheaper room he had booked for himself was on another floor. But they were more or less excited to be together in the city of romance, and he was charmed by her shining eyes and eagerness to be out and about.

They lunched in a nearby restaurant, where the food was too rich for Eugene and the price of it ridiculously high. Immediately afterwards Gloria took him on a two-hour trawl through the shops along the Rue de Rivoli and then into the stores in the Grands Boulevards. She did not buy much, he restrained her from over-spending on their first day; but he was exhausted by five o'clock, said he would rest in his room until dinner time, was too disturbed by the noise

179

of traffic to sleep, and wondered if he had made a mistake in organising such a radical break with everything he was used to.

After dinner in another expensive restaurant they strolled back to the hotel while he took on the difficult task of explaining that love might have to wait for him to replenish his store of energy.

'What a disappointment!' she said, a discouragingly ambiguous reaction – who was disappointed, was she speaking ironically, as if sex was neither here nor there, was she criticising him?

'I shall be a giant refreshed in the morning,' he asserted, and regretted it – he ought not to plead for her pity.

'Will you indeed? I'll hold you to that.'

Was she mocking, was she threatening him?

'I love you very much, Gloria darling.'

'And you're my lovely old boy.'

He hated to be patronised. He had knowledge of the superior airs of women whose men fail to prove that they are made to be on top. He felt under pressure to perform in due course, and at the same time, and really for the first time, that he might experience difficulty.

He spent a restless night. In the morning he let Gloria go shopping alone, and read the English newspapers with relief. In the afternoon she urged him to rest, she was

180

dead set on returning to have a second look at the clothes she thought of buying, expensive though they were. They met at teatime, and then for dinner in yet another restaurant selling indigestible food at exorbitant prices.

Back at the hotel, at the door to her bedroom, she reached up to kiss him lightly and to whisper: 'Come and say good night in a quarter of an hour.'

He changed into his pyjamas, put on his overcoat, and did as he was told, braced to meet strangers on the stairs and for the ordeal in store.

She was already in bed and welcomed him with a smile. He divested himself of his overcoat, preparatory to joining her in the narrow bed; but she said, 'Not like that,' lifted the covers to show him that she had nothing on, and indicated that he was to follow her example and strip to the buff. He did so. They embraced. She was deliciously willing, but he seemed to have been turned to stone. Her efforts to revivify him were counterproductive, her expertise struck him as shocking, he experienced regret after regret, and longed in secret only to escape.

She desisted, gave up, and said, 'You're tired.'

He could not deny it, although her tone was not very sympathetic.

'Go and get some sleep, poor Eugene.'

He controlled his urge to assert himself, and opted for humility.

'It's all my fault,' he said.

'Thanks,' she returned with definite sarcasm.

He climbed into his pyjamas and donned his overcoat.

'You're the most wonderful woman I've ever known,' he said.

She laughed at him unkindly and retorted: 'I'm glad not to be just one of the others, whoever they were.'

'It's never happened to me before,' he claimed.

'Good night, Eugene – don't worry – we'll have fun tomorrow – I mean in the shops.'

He was not happy. He had something else to dread, the bill for her shopping. His comfort was that there were only Friday and Saturday to get through before he would be back at Peters Place.

His foresight in the commercial rather than the sexual context was not erroneous. On Friday he was led like a lamb to the slaughter in the Galeries Lafayette and even in the Rue St Honoré. He paid for her purchases – he felt, and was made to feel, that he had to compensate for having humiliated or at least embarrassed his companion who was not his mistress.

That evening they parted with kisses on cheeks. The next morning cost Eugene another not so small fortune. But after lunch he rebelled and told Gloria to shop on her own – he intended to put his feet up at the hotel. She looked downcast and hostile, so he relented so far as to give her all his folding money and regain a degree of favour.

They met again at seven o'clock, and she surprised him with the warmth of her greeting and the news that she had invited a third party to join them for dinner. She hoped he would not mind, but was not apologetic. She explained that the party in question was the owner of a dress shop in the Rue St Honoré, who had slashed his prices for her and to whom she was indebted – his name was Maurice and he spoke English.

Maurice arrived. He was thirtyish, small, with oiled and crinkly black hair, and the jacket of his suit was waisted and had pockets in unexpected places. He bowed as he shook hands with Eugene, whom he addressed as 'Sir Peter'.

They adjourned to a restaurant recommended by Maurice: it was even more expensive than those in which Eugene had been paying bills. To say that Maurice spoke English was inaccurate – he spoke a lot, using occasionally recognisable English words. His conversation consisted almost entirely of scandalous tales of the behaviour of his female customers, who, he alleged, propositioned him when he took their measurements and carried on in his cubicles.

'Women are *terrible*, *n'est-ce-pas*, Sir Peter?' he asked, flashing his black eyes at Eugene.

He flashed his eyes at Gloria, too. She laughed at his jokes and clearly enjoyed his company: which, Eugene reflected, was better than a gloomy meal for two. At least Gloria did not prolong the meal – she mentioned tomorrow's travel for herself and Eugene, and walked briskly back to the hotel, kissed Maurice good night in the street and kissed Eugene similarly upstairs.

The train journey to London was the last straw in amorous terms for Eugene. Gloria was looking different, he had noticed it before they left the Chateaubriand, more relaxed if tireder, smiling sweetly again in spite of the darker shadows round her eyes. In the train she said a fond farewell to Paris, then thanked Eugene for having given her a wonderful time – she squeezed his arm and twitched her nose at him.

'I'm afraid...' he began to say.

She would not let him end the sentence.

'Don't,' she interrupted. 'That doesn't matter – you're pretty unusual because it hadn't happened to you before – I've no complaints – none at all.'

He guessed then that Maurice had been roped in to subsidise for himself. After dinner the previous evening Gloria had hurried to prepare for the ultimate fitting by the shopkeeper – she was another of the women described by Maurice over dinner. She was considering not Eugene's repose in bed but Maurice's and her own exertions.

Eugene was mortified, he was miserable. He had been superseded – another horrid new experience, for which he had paid more than he could afford. And his successful rival was younger, but half his size, oily, vulgar, foreign and unimportant. He was the biter bit with a vengeance.

He stiffened his upper lip and hoped to save his face by saying to Gloria: 'Thank you, I must thank you, for your great generosity.'

At home, at last, he fished out the cross, and the day after his return he sold it to Barry Hines, the Chipping Sodbury jeweller, for two thousand five hundred pounds. He set aside a hundred of those pounds for Ingram, and presented Mona – and bribed her to forgive him – with four hundred. The rest he paid into his depleted bank account without delay.

Mona thanked him and referred to his business in Paris.

'Any luck there?'

'None to speak of,' he replied.

Rich and Poor

One week after Sir Eugene Peters sold the crucifix, Theodora Leonard-Mickle walked into the jewellery shop in Chipping Sodbury and bought it for three thousand five hundred pounds with her credit card.

Theodora, known as Dora, was the owner of Doddington Place, a large house built in the stockbroker's Tudor style in the 1930s, and located on the Bath side of Lower Sodbury. Doddington Place and its fifty acres almost marched with the lands of stately Doddington Park, built for the Codrington family by the architect James Wyatt on a site landscaped by Capability Brown. The cheekiness of the name of the more modern dwelling in such close proximity to the Codringtons' ancestral pile was still a local scandal.

The builder of Dora's home was her late father, Ira Leonard, one of those brilliant men who hit on or stumble across a way of making a great deal of money in a short space of time. He bought a literal gold mine in some obscure corner of the globe, and was translated from a bank clerk into a magnate in a matter of months. He ran through a wife or two, and late in life wed his secretary, Marian, who bore him an only child, Dora. He then died when Dora was in her teens, leaving her a large inheritance, but less than it might have been. His character was flamboyant and reckless, and some of his investments were as bad as the first one was good.

Dora doted on her father, but did not make him happy. He was sad, for one thing, to see that she was and would be plain, even ugly. She had a big nose, a receding chin, small eyes, a muddy complexion, lank and greasy hair, and was awkwardly put together with her long body, short legs and wide hips. Secondly, she was a disruptive influence. She disliked her mother from day one, refused to be breast-fed, was jealous of Marian for being her father's wife, scratched her, quarrelled with her, ambushed her, and complained of her until Ira in his old age was not sorry to be about to die. Thirdly, she had an insatiable appetite for affection and reassurance: which Ira himself could scarcely supply, and knew that she would find even harder to get in adulthood. Finally, she was wilful, stubborn, deaf to reasoning, and did her best to conceal her better qualities, her religious inclinations, her brain-power and individuality.

In short, Dora hurried and worried Ira Leonard into his grave. She was nineteen and rich. But she had nothing to do and no prospects – her father had been her everything. Marian, his widow, was afraid of her – anyway, Dora would not have co-operated with any suggestion from that quarter. Shyness, the self-consciousness of knowing she was neither pretty nor nice, kept her at home. She bought pets and lost interest in them. She tried to ride horses and fell off. She went to public dos, the Three Day Event at Badminton, the Meets of Hunts, auctions and open days, and met no one worth mentioning. She was not popular in shops, or with new staff. She was very nearly that person who is said not to exist, a friendless person. She consulted psychologists and fortune-tellers. She sought help from the Reverend Archibald Timbrill, then Rector of Sodbury on the Hill with additional responsibilities for Lower Sodbury and Little Sodbury; but he was too strict to suit her. She participated in Retreats in religious houses.

And time passed. She would not lower herself so far as to sign on with a dating agency or advertise for a soulmate, and she tried not to count the days. But she was aware that her thirtieth birthday threatened, and that her restlessness was running out of control. She prayed for a miracle without believing in miracles.

Anyway, Guy Mickie turned up. He was a

tree surgeon, a countryman, middle-class, well-spoken, and not bad looking. He looked rather like his yellow Labrador – his colouring was fair, and he carried his fifty-two years with quiet strength and dignity. She needed someone to sort out her acres of woodland, and, for a start, he supplied that need. He told her that he was a widower when she provided a cup of tea at midday, and she invited him into the house for a drink after he had finished work.

He somehow gave her the confidence to pursue him without hesitation or shame. He was polite, he did not rebuff her – no doubt he was lonely too. She invited him to dinner on three occasions, and would not hear of him leaving her early. On the third occasion he said goodbye at midnight or thereabouts and thanked her again for her kindness.

'Spare me,' she snapped at him.

'I beg your pardon...'

'I've heard that before, thanks and stuff – now I'm waiting.'

'Excuse me, waiting for...'

'Don't be dense, Guy!'

'I'm sorry, but...'

'Well, remember, don't you ever forget, that you forced me to take matters into my own hands!'

She seized him, kissed him, wrestled him on to a sofa and was all over him, telling him she loved him, wanted him, and cursing him for having been so sluggish.

They married in the church at Tormarton, near the cottage where he had continued to live after the death of Joy, his first wife. It was bigger than the Lower Sodbury church; he seemed to have enough friends to fill it; and she had fallen out with Archie Timbrill. Guy had given her an engagement ring of a small garnet set in silver. Dora gave him five thousand pounds under pressure from her solicitor, who said it would be difficult for her to have a penniless husband working a full five-day week. They honeymooned in Stroud, and settled back in Doddington Place.

She worshipped him. His twenty-two years of seniority meant to her that he at least had experience of marital rites. She wanted him in every way at all hours of the days and nights. She became pregnant and bore a daughter, Griselda. But the post-natal effects on her and her marriage were abysmal. To state that she went off Guy would be a euphemism reinforced by a lie. She could not bear him, but utilised him impatiently and coldly in her lustful moods. The trouble was that, whether or not she was fully cognisant of it, on second thoughts she had no respect for a man who could pretend to love, to return the love, of a woman as ill-favoured as she was.

She was bored by him. She called him a

dunce. She hated his slow professional talk and wished every tree in the world would vanish into another dimension. She despised him for letting him dominate her. She despised him again for not being half the man her father had been. And she was angry with him for the problems he began to create.

Dora had exiled her mother to a cottage on the estate, and did not see or talk to her if she could help it. Guy immediately forged a friendly link, and possibly a hostile alliance, with Marian, his mother-in-law. He was a dutiful son as well as a decent son-in-law – he had a crone of a mother, whom he persuaded Dora to visit occasionally and once to invite to stay at Doddington Place. And he had won the apparently exclusive love of Grisel, their daughter, the child she had born with difficulty, who repulsed her ungratefully.

Of course Dora did not care for Grisel. Luckily Grisel was unattractive with her puppy fat and hacking cough – a miniature version of all that she disliked about herself. But Dora's dread was that Grisel might grow to be like Guy and inherit his fine features and enviable complexion. She could not bear the idea of becoming the hideous and pathetic parent of a fashion plate.

Time passed at variable speeds for Dora Leonard-Mickie of Doddington Place. It

192

almost stood still while she waited for something good to happen to her; but it seemed to rush to drag Grisel up and to turn Guy into an old man. Grisel was ten years old in a matter of moments, Dora lamented, and, on top of that, Guy was not always able to do the bidding of her imperious flesh. She could not get over her bad luck, or, in her warm house, with her faithful husband and bright daughter and servants, with her health and her income, the unfairness of her life to date.

She became hypochondriacal and haunted doctors' surgeries. She unearthed psychiatrists who had not yet heard her tales of woe. She thought of converting to Roman Catholicism, or else of becoming a Buddhist. She despaired of God, of His existence, yet night after night, sleepless and dissatisfied, she addressed to Him this rhetorical question in her unspoken prayers:

'Do I deserve it?'

At length this unhappy woman found herself at her fiftieth birthday party. Guy aged seventy-two had arranged it against her will. Grisel was absent, which was one thing to be thankful for. Grisel was now nineteen and prettier than her mother had ever been: she was doing voluntary work in South America – Dora called it beachcombing. The guests were to be Eugene Peters and his Mona,

193

Piers de Bray, a group of medical personnel, and Dora's mother Marian. Guy's birthday present had been a Locust Tree sapling, *Robinia pseudoacacia*, the False Acacia, and she had cried when she saw it, which he took to be a compliment.

The guests were invited for six-thirty in the evening, a Friday evening. The weather was atrocious – heavy rain for the fourth day in succession – and the prelude to the party was typical of the Leonard-Mickies in that things went from bad to worse.

Dora was put out that Guy had asked Marian to join them. While he opened a bottle of champagne behind the screen in the sitting-room, she upbraided him for subjecting her to the company of her mother: 'You know I loathe her.' He shook his head sadly and called her 'dear': 'That isn't natural, dear' – to which she objected with a scowl and a muttered expletive.

Guy then served three glasses of champagne on a tray, and he and Marian drank a toast to Dora.

'Thank you, but I wish you hadn't,' she snapped.

Guy, talking to Marian, launched into a disquisition about his present. Dora interrupted him: 'For God's sake, Guy!' Marian said how sorry she was that the daughter of the house could not be present. Dora commented, 'I'm glad, if you want to know.'

194

Marian dared to protest: 'Why are you always so sharp with me?' Dora said: 'I didn't ask you to come here. If you choose to take it on the chin, that's not my fault.' Marian cried and addressed Guy: 'You're married to a cruel woman.' He said: 'She doesn't mean it, Marian.' And Dora contradicted him: 'I do, I do!'

Marian fled. Guy remonstrated with the birthday girl, who told him to shut up. Guy said: 'We're too old for these rows, Dora.' She replied: 'Fiddlesticks,' and walked out of the room.

The guests arrived. Although Dora joined them, she did not exactly join in. The atmosphere was sticky, and the hostess made it all too clear that she was feeling inhospitable and longed to be alone. A couple of remarks impressed her more than the rest of the predictable babble. Piers de Bray told her the sweetest little lie, that she looked better with every passing year whereas everybody else looked worse. And when Eugene Peters wished her luck, and she replied that she could do with it, he mentioned the crucifix, which was reputed to be lucky, although he did not believe in such nonsense, and revealed that he had owned it and disposed of it in Chipping Sodbury.

The next day Dora received a letter from the agent in charge of her investment in the Lloyd's Insurance Market, informing her that she owed a sum of money so large that she could not comprehend the figures.

She called to Guy – she was in her dining-room, about to eat breakfast – and he was still upstairs. He called back that he was on his way, but delayed as usual, and she screamed at him:

'Hurry up, you old fool!'

He arrived, flustered. She thrust the letter into his shaky hands, saying: 'Read it, read it – I'm ruined!'

He put on his spectacles, came in for more abuse, stared at the letter, let it fall to the ground, uttered a cry of pain, collapsed slowly on to the floor, and lost consciousness.

She began several sentences: 'What the hell... What do you think you're... Guy, stop... Oh, for God's sake, don't do this to me!'

She knelt down. His stertorous breathing alarmed her. She shook him, she slapped his discoloured hands. She realised at last that he was very ill, struggled in a rush to get to her feet, crashed the back of her head into the underside of the oak sideboard, saw stars and toppled over herself.

She did not pass out, but her head swam and ached and her sight was affected. She pushed and pulled herself into the upright. Her legs wobbled, her knees were surely knocking, but she made it into the kitchen, where her housekeeper Edith sat her in a chair and coped with ringing for an ambulance.

Guy was taken to Frenchay Hospital in Bristol. Dora did not feel fit enough to visit him until later in the day – Edith drove her. He was in Intensive Care, had had a severe heart attack, was all wired up, and turned his head away when he caught sight of her. She did not stay long.

She was startled and hurt by that movement of his head. He had relented, vouchsafed a smile at her belatedly, but had nothing to say. She returned to Doddington Place at five o'clock, and in the next forty-odd hours underwent a type of transformation.

For good reasons or bad selfish ones, and possibly because she had been concussed, she decided that she could not lose her money and her husband at the same time. Where would she be, what would she be, without her wealth? She had been able to afford to look down on people who, in one respect, were more fortunate than she was, that is less ugly and less repulsive. Unprotected by her money, she would either have to become a tramp, a bag-lady, or make peace with the rest of the world. The same applied to Guy: he was better than nothing, for she feared that at fifty, and at fifty without a fortune, she would never find another man, let alone a consort. She must cease to bully him. She must not let him slip through her fingers by default. He had enraged her not so long ago by regretting the fact that she was spoilt. Untrue, she had yelled. He was not to cast aspersions on her father, she bellowed. But, after all, she could vaguely see that it was a fact. Her beloved father should not have allowed her to contract the habit of tormenting his wife, her mother Marian. She herself should have treated her mother in line with the Commandments of God, and she never should have allowed her relations with Grisel to deteriorate pretty well to vanishing point.

On the Sunday of that weekend with its traditional trio of horrid accidents Dora went to Matins in Chipping Sodbury. She was penitent. She was sorry for her life. She wished she was entitled to confess her sins and obtain absolution. She begged the Almighty to hear her prayers, as He never had before. Let Guy survive, she pleaded. Make me better than I have been, she implored. Prevent Lloyd's from taking all my money – leave me some, she entreated. Forgive me, and allow me to stay in Doddington Place. Teach me to be nice to my mother, and how to win Grisel's love, not her hatred. Please do not punish me any more for being spoilt – I will give a lot of the money I am left with to Your church, I promise.

After the service, as she drove on to

Frenchay Hospital to check that Guy was alive, she noticed the shop of Barry Hines, the jeweller; and on the Monday morning she bought the crucifix.

Her bruised head was better. Her losses incurred at Lloyd's proved to be less ruinous than had seemed to be the case. Guy recovered sufficiently to be released from hospital. Grisel came home. And Dora wondered if she was the beneficiary of blessings in disguise, or, with reservations, if the crucifix could have something to do with these developments.

On the day after Guy's return to Doddington Place, while she sat near him in the drawing-room, she overcame the difficulty of communicating verbally by holding his hand.

'Thank you,' he said slowly – he was slowed to a snail's pace by his illness.

'I'm glad you're with me again,' she declared.

'Are you?'

'I'm sorry for not treating you well. Can you hear me?'

'Just.'

'Forgive me if you can. I'll be as nice as I can be from now on.'

'Fancy that!'

'Do you forgive me, Guy?'

'What?'

She had to repeat herself.

'There, there,' he said.

In her new mood she could control her impatience and scorn of his thick-headedness; and as for the unconscious humour of some of their exchanges, she had never looked for or seen the funny side of things.

She sought a reconciliation with her mother, although Marian had reacted badly to the family crisis, locked herself away in the cottage she occupied, and was not always clear in the head.

Marian, after eventually opening the cottage door, began by asking if Dora was getting well again.

'I haven't been ill,' Dora replied, 'it's Guy who's been ill.'

'No wonder!'

Dora said defensively: 'He's in his seventy-third year, Mother. But I haven't come about that.'

'Is it the money.'

'What?'

'You're not going to turn me out into the streets, Dora, now you're poor?'

'Certainly not.'

'It would be wicked.'

'I'm not going to do it.'

'Oh I do hope not!'

'Mother, I've come to say how sorry I am – I know I've been beastly to you.'

'Oh you have, Dora. I could tell you

stories to prove how beastly you've been.'

'Please don't! I've turned over a new leaf. I feel I've become a different person.'

'Who are you then?'

'No, Mother. Please forgive me. I'm awfully sorry.'

'That's a relief.'

'Do you understand, Mother?'

'Yes, dear. Well, I'll wait and see. Will you keep it up?'

'I'm going to try.'

Dora did her best to grin and bear the maternal reproaches, which were disagreeably emphasised by her guilty conscience.

In response to Dora's contrite approach, Grisel inquired: 'What's the big idea, Mother?'

Dora told her.

'I don't believe it,' Grisel said. 'But I suppose it's a step in the right direction.'

'I'm ashamed of myself, and I understand why you've been against me.'

'I was for Dad, for Dad and yours truly – to say I was against you is half the story.'

'You were always prettier than me, and everyone was fond of you – I envied you and wasn't generous.'

'Wrong again, Mother – I'm not worth envying, and not everyone's fond of me.'

'What do you mean? What's happened to you? I'm sorry – I've only been thinking of myself.'

'Don't worry – it doesn't matter – it never has mattered – you won't be interested.'

Dora denied it. After a short argument Grisel confessed that she was unhappy, having been given the push by her Peruvian lover – which made Dora happier. Mother and daughter went on to share confidences. Dora suggested that a street vendor in Lima might never fit in at Lower Sodbury. Grisel said she was so glad to see that Dora was at last caring for Guy as he deserved. And they discussed the pivotal problem of their looks.

Grisel, either tactfully or without meaning to please her mother, complained of her hair – too fine, mousey and English – and said she was embarrassed by the heaviness of her breasts and the width of her hips.

'Don't talk of hips to me,' Dora sighed.

'I could give birth to a toddler,' Grisel said.

They met as friends on the common female ground of men and how to deal with them. Dora revealed the disappointments of her youth and of not being married, and then of her marriage to dear unromantic Guy. Grisel, in return, confided that sexually she was inhibited or something – her boyfriends all told her so.

'I'm the wrong woman to counsel you,' Dora was sorry to say, and Grisel cheered her up by claiming that she would have been disgusted if her mother had initiated her into vicious practices and taught her squalid tricks.

One day Dora showed Grisel the crucifix.

'What are you going to do with it?' her daughter asked.

'It's not like that, it's the opposite – I bought it because of what it might do with me and for me.'

'Has it done anything?'

'Well – I like to think my home's turning into a proper family home for a change. Guy's on the mend, you're here, and I've never felt so content as I do now. The thing's meant to be lucky, you see.'

'It's religious, isn't it?'

'Yes. I bought it for that reason too.'

'I wish I was religious,' Grisel said.

Dora replied: 'I haven't been a good Christian. I don't deserve to be forgiven. But I'm sort of on the way to forgiving God.'

Grisel, inattentively, changed the subject.

'You could wear that crucifix – crosses are all the rage.'

On another day Dora said she found life easier since she had renounced sex and retreated from the battle of the sexes.

Grisel said: 'You're only fifty, Mother – you must fly the flag, even though Dad's going to be an invalid from now on. You never know what's over the horizon.'

'Oh but I do, darling. Look at me! My face

is past praying for, and I'd prefer to draw a veil across my body.'

'You could have a face-lift,' Grisel said.

In a matter of days Dora overcame her scruples. She was excited by the prospect of having her face lifted, as pretty people did. She hoped to look like a new woman as well as feeling like one, and she was keen to cement her bond with Grisel by following her advice.

She fixed an appointment with Dr Wood in Chipping Sodbury and went to see him one afternoon with Grisel in tow and in command. She had not informed Guy, who was a puritan and would have disapproved of even such an innocuous preliminary inquiry. She had been assured by Grisel that Guy would not notice the planned alterations. She was relieved on that score, while secretly imagining the joy of his discovering how much better-looking she had become.

Dr Wood was old, had known Dora since she was a girl, and had been in at the birth of Grisel.

He poured cold water on the scheme.

'Why, Dora? You look well to me. I like to see nature in a face. Who do you think will benefit, apart from the butcher boys? There can be unintended consequences, remember. Griselda, you should be restraining your mother. My opinion is, don't do it.'

Dora was taken aback. Grisel contradicted Dr Wood for her mother's sake. At length he consented to supply the names of a pair of plastic surgeons, one in Harley Street, the other in Bristol.

Mother and daughter took a day trip to London. Mr Marcus Tregonning kept them waiting for an hour, wore a carnation in his buttonhole, said he would charge ten thousand pounds to correct Dora's facial defects, and, for all three reasons, was rejected. In Bristol they consulted Mr Angus Macswinn, who said Dora's face was a huge challenge, but he did not mind having a slash at it for roughly the same sum quoted by Mr Tregonning.

In the old days Dora would have called the surgeons sharks and consigned them publicly or privately to hell. Now she was set on getting her way, which would fill her bowl of happiness to the brim. Besides, Grisel was planning to return to her Peruvian lover, who had been pressing his suit with e-mails, and was determined to put her theory into practice with the minimum delay.

Dora heard of a plastic surgeon in Yate, Mr Simon Cowdray. Her housekeeper Edith's son, Howard, had had an unsightly mole removed from the middle of his forehead by Mr Cowdray, leaving no visible scar. A brief visit to Mr Cowdray's premises sealed the deal: he would remove wrinkles from the upper half of Dora's countenance, shrink the bags under her eyes, rearrange her jaw line, and pin up the flesh under her chin, all for two thousand pounds in cash. Dora was delighted with Simon, as she was asked to call him in the course of that first visit – he was so handsome and keen and she was pleased to think she had struck a hard bargain considering the state of her finances.

She told Guy she was going to have a minor woman's operation, which was not too far from the truth. She left him in charge of Grisel, and on the appointed day clocked in at a small nursing home in Bristol. She had taken the crucifix with her and two thousand pounds in notes. She was more excited than fearful, and held the crucifix and thanked God for her many blessings, especially the one about to change her appearance and perhaps her destiny. Her anaesthetic was general and the operation lasted for three and a half hours. She was all bandaged up when she came round, and was not allowed a mirror when her wounds were dressed and re-bandaged.

Grisel was in attendance on the day that Dora looked at herself. Perhaps against expectations, since Simon Cowdray was both young and cheap, the consensus was favourable. Scars were still visible, but the medical prognosis was that they would fade. Grisel was thrilled and Dora was persuaded that she had done the right thing. Admittedly, her heightened eyebrows gave her a startled expression. Her right eye refused to blink, and her lips were thinner and wider than they had been; but her new face was different from and therefore better than her old one, and she hoped that in time others would prefer it.

The next challenge was to show it to Guy and Edith and co. at Doddington Place. Grisel helped her to apply make-up for the first time. Guy hit the right note by saying he could see that her operation had done her a power of good, and Edith followed suit, if with veiled reservations.

Grisel departed for Peru, promising to return, possibly with her Peruvian, in a few months. Guy was less sad to bid his daughter goodbye than he would have been in the bad old days, when his wife was unkind to him. Similarly Dora, who begged Grisel not to stay away too long, had compensations in the form of knowing that she was no longer a hopelessly ugly duckling.

At this point Dora's spirits soared – it was as if they were making up for having been depressed for half a century. She thanked God for leading her, if slowly, into an enchanted garden where she could be appreciated and admired. She smiled, she sang, and, although she took most of the credit for the improvements of her lot, she acknowledged that the crucifix had some-how contributed. Two ideas occurred to her, one that she might wear it, the other that she might find and finance a replacement for the missing jewel.

She did hesitate: would it be sacrilege to turn the crucifix into an adornment? Would it be wrong to hang it between her breasts? And what was she to add to it that would be sufficiently holy – especially as she hoped it might attract a roving male eye? But she was not in the mood for self-restraint, and hurried to Chipping Sodbury to discuss the matter with Barry Hines.

Barry's notions were the opposite of godly. He said he had wanted to repair the crucifix after buying it from Sir Eugene Peters, and would now do the repair for Dora at cost price. He thought either that the hole should be filled in with silver and added to a chain of numerous lucky charms, or that it should be plugged with gold on which Dora's initials were engraved. Unfortunately Barry was a professional jeweller, that is persuasive, and Dora still lacked confidence in her taste. She plumped for the golden option, and worried that the crucifix would be defaced.

That night she had a bad dream. She dreamt that her head was infested with lice, and woke and touched her hair, which was wet. She switched on the light. Her pillow was blood red – she was bleeding profusely from a wound in her hairline – the scar of one of Simon Cowdray's incisions had burst open.

It was three in the morning. Dora roused Edith, who, disturbingly, guessed at once what had happened, and they rang for an ambulance. Edith promised to break the news gently to Guy in the morning, and Dora was taken to the Accident and Emergency Unit at Frenchay Hospital, operated on and kept in a General Ward until the next day.

Edith fetched her. Edith gasped at the sight of her. The skin stretched and sewn to Dora's scalp had slipped downwards. It almost covered her left eye, and her whole left cheek seemed to hang loosely, bulging out and spreading over her jaw. Her mouth had gone awry, flapping open on that side.

Edith cried, Dora cried.

Dora said: 'I've been wicked.'

Edith was puzzled and shook her head.

'Edith, do something for me, please. Ring Barry Hines, you know, the jeweller in Chipping, and tell him not to touch the crucifix – not to touch it – will you do that for me?'

'Yes, yes, I will – but now, what now?'

'Take me to the Nursing Home where I was before, and ask Dr Wood to come and see me without delay.'

'What's the crucifix got to do with this?'

'Everything,' Dora said.

Believe it or Not

The five Sodburys fared differently in December's weather. Sodbury on the Hill was beset by at least two of the four winds, the one coming approximately from the west, from Ireland and the Atlantic, curling over the escarpment and threatening to blow its houses down, and the one from the east, from Russia, trying to root it up and tip it over and into the Vale below. All the winds whined mournfully round the corners of Peters Place, where Sir Eugene dreamed of the loves he had lost, and the new owner of The Grange, who had bought it from Dolf Colquhoun, wished that Aaron Colquhoun had used more brick than glass in its construction. At Sodbury Holding the cows munching the cud must have strained their ears to hear if the fresh green grass was growing in response to the rainfall.

Little Sodbury on the hillside was exposed fully frontally to the winds whirling up the Severn Channel, whereas Old Sodbury and Chipping Sodbury both benefited from their locations at the lower level. In return for having no long views, they were less wind-swept in winter and a degree or two warmer.

No snow had fallen yet to disguise the ugliness of Fred Croggett's dump of motor machinery. But, as the temperature fell, the shed in the garden of the Sheep and Goats at Lower Sodbury was used less for immoral purposes since it was unheated and draughty.

Half a mile from the village of Lower Sodbury, which was and would have been a hamlet but for its little church, a picturesque thatched cottage crouched beyond a garden and a picket fence. It denied that it was a bungalow by means of a tiny dormer window peeping through the thickness of the thatch; but actually the accommodation was a sitting-room behind the front door, a room on the left with a single bed in it, a slip of a kitchen behind the bedroom, and an extension with a corrugated iron roof housing lavatory, wash-basin and bath. A ladder rather than a staircase in the sitting-room led to a low and confined attic space.

It was the home of the Reverend Archibald Timbrill, formerly the Rector of Sodbury on the Hill, Little Sodbury and Lower Sodbury, now in his eighties and retired, though occasionally called upon to conduct a service or to help with the Communion at local churches.

He had lived in the Sodbury area for forty years. He hailed from the North of England, had been a minister in various northern towns, then married and was appointed to

212

the West Country job. His wife was called Jean. He loved her dearly, they were as happy as their days were long, dwelt in the Sodbury on the Hill Rectory, and had one child, a daughter, Sally. But Jean died first, much to his disappointment, and Sally married an Australian and went to live in Melbourne. He was not quite alone for a time thereafter: his sister Ellen had bought and come to live in Sunnyside, the thatched cottage already described. It was when he was deserted by Ellen, who also predeceased him against his will, that he retired, vacated his overlarge Rectory and moved into her home.

Archie Timbrill had good health of the most obstinate kind, as he often described it to himself. He had been prepared to die years ago, but death avoided him, death cut him almost rudely, and he obeyed the will of God and dutifully enjoyed the extra year after year of life that he was granted. He was of medium build, well-proportioned, with an equable temperament and common sense, as men with the strongest constitutions usually are. The call he had received to become a priest may be inexplicable; but his faith in Christianity, his devotion to his 'cure' of souls, the selflessness of his character, and the charm and lovability of his personality, were recognised by all and sundry in the neighbourhood.

He became a gardener in his older age. He

grew cottage flowers from packets of seeds in his front garden, and a few vegetables in the patch at the back. He had the patience for it, was born with patience and probably developed it in his experience of the slow grinding of the mills of God, and his affection for his plants seemed to please them. He had some white hair left, it grew across the crown of his head, and his clear yet weathered complexion derived not only from his practical gardening, but also from the bench against the cottage wall and the two deck chairs in a sheltered spot, where he would sit, contemplate, read, and entertain his visitors.

He was not allowed much leisure in which to till the soil or rest in his own quiet way. Retirement had proved to be a synonym for business as usual in his case. To begin with, he was in charge of the Lower Sodbury church and was the keeper of the key to its door. Then, because he had made so many friends in the other Sodburys, he was now begged to confirm or marry their children, or christen their grandchildren, or bury them. Word of mouth brought him a host of new applicants for his guidance, his blessings and the possibly healing touch of his hands. He was said to be a saint: he laughed at the people who called him saintly to his face. He was against such silly gossip and exaggeration. He sternly assured his admirers that he was ordinary, nothing to write home about, still struggling not to make mistakes, and, in a word, a servant, theirs and God's.

The irreligion of the age, and the paganism, passed Archie Timbrill by. His contention was that he only had to scratch an atheist or an agnostic, metaphorically, in order to reveal a knowingly or unknowingly religious spirit. Cleverer people ascribed his influential power to his sincerity. It was all in his eyes, according to innocence and ignorance. The simple truth, which is never simplistic, was that he was intelligent, unpretentious, receptive, responsive, not a snob, not a bigot, and made everyone feel good or at least better.

He had a telephone in Sunnyside – it was needed. The cottage was isolated in its lane; but Archie walked into Lower Sodbury on most days to open and air the church, to clean it and pray, and once or twice a week to catch the bus into Chipping. He possessed no car or bicycle. He was fetched by the Verger or Churchwarden of a church where he was required to officiate, and petitioners of one sort and another drove to Sunnyside and parked by the picket fence. He was never lonely – he often saw his Lower Sodbury neighbours or they saw him, apart from visitors from farther afield – and in his solitude he had superior company.

One morning at eight o'clock or there-abouts his telephone rang. He was finishing his breakfast of a slice of buttered toast with honey and two cups of tea. He lifted the receiver and gave his telephone number.

'It's Dora,' the caller said in a muffled tone.

'Excuse me – I couldn't hear you.'

'From Doddington Place – I'm Dora.'

'This is a pleasant surprise, Dora.'

'Can I come and talk to you?'

'Please do. When would suit you?'

'It must be the other way round. When can you spare the time?'

'This morning, if you like.'

'I'm sorry I've been... I've been such a bad neighbour.'

'I'm sorry for the same reason, Dora.'

'Will you... Will you be prepared...? I'm different now.'

'It'll be all right. Come at eleven, or I could come to you.'

'Thank you so much.'

'Which is it to be?'

'I'll drive down.'

Dora Leonard-Mickie arrived at Sunnyside at eleven-fifteen. It was a grey day but dry, and Archie opened his front door and walked along the path to meet her. He wore cor-duroy trousers, a jersey and his dog-collar.

Dora delayed. After a pause she stepped

out of her car. She wore a head scarf and dark sunglasses although there was no sun. She shook Archie's outstretched hand almost in passing, and she swept past him and towards the cottage. He followed her into his sitting-room, where a fire of sticks burned in the grate, and she seated herself on a chair beside it with her back to the light admitted by a small window somewhat overgrown by greenery.

'Can I offer you a cup of tea or coffee, Dora?'

'Nothing, thanks.'

'Would you like me to take your coat and scarf?'

'No.'

'I'm very pleased to see you again. Thank you for coming. I'm sorry I offended you when we used to meet and talk.'

'You were right.'

'And wrong.' He paused and asked her: 'What brings you here?'

'It's difficult,' she said in a voice that quavered.

'I've enough time. Don't hurry. Is it illness?'

'I can't say that.'

'Dora, am I visible through your glasses?'

'It is illness in a way.'

'Your husband Guy is better, I understand?'

'Yes. Yes, but... But I'm disfigured.'

'Tell me whatever you want to tell me. I

217

won't interrogate you. I sympathise with your unhappiness.'

'You advised me not to be discontented. I didn't follow your advice. I couldn't. You won't know what I mean – men don't know – my father didn't know. My life's been a stupid mess, but I'm clever enough to see how stupid it's been. I was made not of all things nice – I wasn't made of the right stuff for girls – I had religious inklings and was romantic – and my face turned those ingredients sour and they poisoned me.'

She cried.

He let her cry, then said: 'I'm listening.'

'You wouldn't know how terrible it is to be too ugly to be loved by the men you're able and willing to love. The shock of discovering that young men were not like Daddy, who always thought I was perfect, was so destructive... I hated God, which was exactly the opposite of my other intentions and yearnings. Oh yes, I married Guy, but my heart wasn't in it. I had a daughter, Griselda, as well as a husband, but they were never the objects, the people, I desired. I'm not proud of any of this, Archie – to say it is to show you what a wreck I became, what a wreck I am. But it's all beside the point.'

'What is the point?'

'Not long ago I bought something from Barry Hines, the jeweller in Chipping Sodbury. Eugene Peters, you know him, told me it was magical, a charm doling out good luck and perhaps bad luck too. Well... Well, Guy recovered from his heart attack, Grisel became my friend rather than an appendage and a reminder that she was no love-child, and everything changed. I regained the confidence of my girlhood, I felt I could nearly move mountains, and by my own efforts cancel the curse that had been laid upon me. Sorry to be so slow!'

'It's all right.'

'I had my face lifted. The result was wonderful. But I had doubts about having had it done and, more, about having it done cheaply and not honestly. On the other hand, even so late in the day, I convinced myself that my prospects were improving. I blundered on, and sought out Barry Hines and agreed to let him fiddle with my cross, my luck. How crazy! How crass! I see it now – as usual, too late! The operation went wrong. A scar burst open and half my face collapsed. Who cares?'

She cried again.

'Take off your specs, Dora – I've seen faces more collapsed than yours, I'm sure.'

She removed the glasses. He did not flinch.

He asked: 'Are you getting it readjusted?'

'Yes, some time, when I can afford it.'

'This lucky charm of yours. What was it like?'

'I'm ashamed to tell you.'

'Better tell me, Dora.'

'An old cross.'

'A Christian cross?'

'Yes. I think so. It could be very old... Some people say it's a crucifix. Please don't be angry with me, Archie!'

'I'm not.'

'Are you all right, Archie?'

'Do you still possess the crucifix?'

'Yes–'

'Do you have it with you?'

'Yes–'

'Can I see it, Dora?'

'Yes.'

She fumbled in her bag, produced the crucifix wrapped in tissue paper, proffered it and said: 'I want to give it to our church.'

He unwrapped it and, holding it in his hand, smiled at her with tears welling into his eyes.

'Archie?' she queried uncertainly, fearing that she had upset him or that he was ill.

'Oh Dora,' he returned, and repeated the two words. Then he said in a husky voice: 'You've given me what vindicates my life.'

'I don't see...'

He held out his thin hand, she placed her hand in his, and he stood up, gently pulled her to her feet, and said: 'Come with me.'

He led her out of the cottage and along the lane. She asked questions, but he only answered them by saying, 'Wait – all will be revealed.'

They reached the church. He unlocked the door and led her towards the altar. On the white wall on the left of the altar were two pins side by side. Archie silently and reverently slipped the vertical part of the crucifix between them and lowered it so that the horizontal arms rested precisely on the pins.

He turned to smile at Dora and to say: 'Now you see.'

He then lifted the crucifix off its pins, laid it on the altar, crossed over to a little table standing against the right-hand wall, opened a drawer and extracted a small object, holding it between finger and thumb. He retraced his steps, showed Dora the object, a globular bit of glass resembling a marble, lifted up the crucifix, inserted the glass into its empty aperture, and replaced it.

He said: 'I know this is like a conjuring trick, but it isn't a trick.'

They returned to Sunnyside and talked over cups of tea. He confirmed that the cross was indeed a crucifix, and that her 'bit of glass' was in fact pure crystal and symbolised the head of Jesus. He explained that it had been stolen from Lower Sodbury church just about twelve months ago, and that its return via the kindness of Dora was a boon and a blessing without parallel in his experience.

He said he would spare her the religious lessons implicit in the events of the last half hour, but that, later on, after he had perhaps obtained more information, he might have something else to say on the subject.

She confessed that she had considered having a lump of gold with her initials on it put where the crystal belonged, so that she could hang the crucifix round her neck along with her other jewellery. She added that her punishment, the ruination of half her face, had fitted the crime of her vanity and wrong-headedness.

'Don't be too hard on yourself, Dora. Don't feel guilty. I absolve you in so far as I'm able to. Go and have your face mended. I believe I can promise you that the Almighty in view of your good deed today will see to it that the next operation does you no more harm.'

A week elapsed. It was mid-December, and the days began late and ended early, and the nights were almost as long as they would be on the twenty-first of the month, the shortest day of the year. The ditches filled beside the lane where Sunnyside stood, and when no rain fell the dry leaves rustled in the roadway. On the other hand, snowdrops were already in bloom in the shady part of the Sunnyside garden, and the buds of daffodils were daring to push their heads above ground.

Archie Timbrill was even happier than he was accustomed to being. The crucifix was back where it belonged – it had proved its attachment to Lower Sodbury; and that cause of Archie's extra happiness was reinforced by his attempts to unravel the story of its wanderings. Faith filled the gaps in his researches – his was not a scientific mind, let alone a pedantic one, he was satisfied to see the wood without bothering to count the trees.

On another morning, a Saturday morning, he received two visitors. They were a young man and a young woman in a large newish car, and had not made an appointment. He saw them – had been in his garden – and approached and greeted them as the girl pushed open the gate in the picket fence and the youth limped in after her. She was pretty, a clean-cut brunette with a confident manner; he was slim with a cap of brown hair that curled over his forehead, and wore jeans and a clean short-sleeved shirt without a tie.

'Hi,' they said in chorus in reply to Archie's hullo.

'Are you Mr Timbrill?' the girl demanded.

'Yes, I am.'

'Good morning,' she said more graciously. 'Could we talk to you, sir? We'd like you to marry us.'

'Congratulations!'

The visitors looked nonplussed by Archie's benevolence.

'Come indoors,' he said. 'You'll be cold out here without a coat,' he added to the young man, who shrugged his shoulders by way of denial.

The three of them sat in the front room of Sunnyside – or, rather, Archie sat in one armchair, the girl perched on the edge of the seat of the sofa, and her friend lounged back beside her, perhaps because he had to keep his lame leg fully extended.

'What are your names, may I ask?'

'I'm Marjorie, Marjorie Reynolds, and my boyfriend's Andrew. We're engaged.'

'And now you want to be married?'

Marjorie turned her head to look at Andrew, who mumbled, 'Right!'

'I don't think I know you. Do you live in Lower Sodbury?'

'We're from Tetbury.' Marjorie replied.

'What brings you to our village? Why would you like to be married here?'

'My mother was called Timmins before she married.'

'You're related to the Timmins family who ran the nursery garden?'

'Bob Timmins is my uncle, sir.'

'I begin to see light.'

'And you christened me, sir.'

'Did I? Forgive me for not recognising the

baby I once held in my arms, changed though she is.'

Marjorie and Archie both laughed at the pleasantry. Andrew kept the straightest of faces.

'But I didn't marry your parents?' Archie asked. 'I hope I haven't had another lapse of my memory.'

'They were married in Tetbury. Dad's family are Tetbury people. But Mum wanted me christened where she came from. And she thought a lot of you.'

'Well – please thank her for that. Of course, in theory, I'd be proud to marry you to Andrew; but I don't need to tell you I'm old – I mean that God may have other ideas for me. In practice, I'll marry you if I can. Would it suit you to proceed on that understanding?'

'Yes, definitely. Andrew?'

'Right,' he concurred again.

Archie asked how long they had known each other.

'Just under a year,' Marjorie replied. 'I'm a nurse, and he had the accident, and we met in Tetbury Hospital. We're saving to buy a home in one of the Sodburys.'

'Are you from these parts, Andrew?'

Marjorie answered for him.

'We're going into the taxi business. We've bought our first taxi – it's outside. Andrew's mechanical – he's studied and got his qualifications. And he thinks business would be better here than in Tetbury. He wants to get away from Tetbury.'

'I wish you good luck. Would you like to give me your names, and suggest a possible date for the wedding, I've got a pencil and paper, and even a diary for next year, if you're prepared to wait until after Christmas. Your full names, Marjorie?'

'Marjorie Anne Reynolds.'

Archie wrote and turned to Andrew, who said: 'Matthew Andrew Conley.'

'You use your second Christian name?' Archie queried.

Marjorie answered: 'He does now.'

They discussed dates and fixed one in January of the next year.

'Shall we go along to the church?' Archie suggested. 'I'd like you to have an idea of its size and seating capacity, and you might like me to bless you both while we're there. No obligation – I won't mind if you'd rather not.'

Marjorie was all agreement and enthusiasm. Andrew raised no objections. They inspected the font and counted seats in pews. She loved the building, and he limped up the aisle to receive the blessing.

Then, standing before the altar, Andrew nearly fainted. He staggered, was white in the face, sweated, and had to be helped into a pew.

'What's wrong? What's wrong with you?' Marjorie kept on asking him with concern and a trace of irritation – she was an efficient girl and seemed to expect him to fall in with her plans.

At length he said to her: 'Do me a favour, Marje – give me two minutes with the vicar – I'll explain after – wait outside for two minutes, will you?'

'What's this about?' she rattled.

'No, Marje, not now – wait outside!'

She obeyed him. She made a grimace, flushed, shook her head, but did as she was told.

Andrew then said to Archie: 'It's the cross,' pointing at the crucifix. 'I stole it. How did it get there?'

'Nobody knows. God alone knows.'

'I stole money too.'

'Yes.'

'I'll give it back. It was twenty-nine pounds. I'll give you thirty.'

'Thank you.'

'I'm sorry. I'm not called Matt any more. I don't do bad things no more. But I came over ill when I saw the cross, because I threw it away twelve months ago.'

'Where did you throw it?'

'Into Hetty's Pot. I did a bad thing to it, and it did a bad thing to me. It learned me.'

'What do you mean.'

'I had a crash on my motorbike when I

227

was throwing it into the Pot. I was crocked up all night in a field. It was time to think. I wasn't half afraid of what else the cross might do to me.'

'I have to thank you with all my heart for telling me these things.'

'Here's the thirty, sir.'

'Can you afford it?'

'Sure! I'm earning well, repairing cars and with the taxi work. Thanks for not giving me what-for.'

'I'm thinking of blessing you instead.'

'Marje would love that, and I'd appreciate it, sir, I would.'

'Go and call her in.'

A few days later Archie Timbrill caught the bus in Lower Sodbury for Chipping, and, before doing his shopping, went into Winson's, the newsagent, and received permission from Andy Winson to pin a small card on the noticeboard, amongst the adverts of items for sale and wanted, offers of jobs and pleas for the return of lost kittens.

On his card he had printed the information that on the Sunday before Christmas – date supplied – the Reverend Archibald Timbrill would be preaching during Matins – time supplied – at Lower Sodbury church.

The consequence was that on the morning in question Archie found himself facing almost a full house. Word of the Service had spread through the village; Mrs Williams had gallantly agreed to play the out-of-tune piano in the church; Joe Hunt, the verger, was keen to toll the bell; everybody liked Archie, and a good number of his neighbours attended. Guy and Dora Leonard-Mickie were there, and Eugene Peters and Mona Welby, and Barbara Colquhoun, and Marjorie Reynolds with her mother and her Andrew, formerly Matt. At the back of the church Dan and Peggy Green from Sodbury Holding sat with their new baby and first child, who would shortly be christened Victor Sam by Mr Timbrill.

It was not a nice day – grey cloud, spots of rain, wind blowing up. Perhaps it was typical of Archie therefore to choose *All things bright and beautiful* for his first hymn. Prayers and a psalm led into his sermon. The congregation was seated, a hush fell, he stood in front of the altar, and spoke without notes as follows.

'Good morning. I can hardly claim to be more than the caretaker of this church, so I'm the more grateful to everybody for coming along and waiting to hear a caretaker's words on a subject so great and deep as religion. I'm grateful, besides, to the Reverend Alan Hart, Rector of four of the five Sodbury churches, Sodbury on the Hill, Little and Old, plus Lower, for allowing and encouraging me to conduct today's Matins.

My friend and my boss Alan will be finding time somehow for a Communion Service here on Christmas Day – I'll announce details as soon as I know them and will post a notice in Chipping Sodbury and on our church door.

'To begin with, I am glad to be the harbinger of good news: I am too old to preach to you for long. The second bit of good news is that our crucifix has come home – some of you will be able to see it in place, and I shall now fetch and hold it high.'

He approached the wall on his right, lifted the crucifix from its pins, returned and showed it to the congregation.

'The origins and history of this beautiful object are lost in the mists of time. It was bequeathed to this church in 1872 by a Mrs Bushell, a widow, who had died in London but is thought to have either lived or grown up in Lower Sodbury. Mrs Bushell's husband worked in the East, in India or beyond – we have no documentary evidence in that context. Having received the crucifix we treasured it, and it remained unmolested on the wall over there until earlier this year.

'May I name once again the gemstones inlaid in the metal of the oddly-shaped cross? There are seven, a number of significance reaching back into pre-history, and making appearances throughout the Old Testament. In my opinion, the seven factor is merely a linking of Christianity with Judaism and Jewry and the religions of the more distant past. Now, starting at the top of the upright, we have rock crystal, secondly amethyst, thirdly peridot – clear, purple and green. The four gemstones from left to right on either side of the central amethyst are rose beryl, yellow citrine, blue natural topaz, red garnet. Altogether they form a representation of Jesus, typical of the age when it would have been sacrilegious to try to portray the flesh and blood of the Son of God. The amethyst is a metaphor for the heart, the clear crystal for the head, and the other stones for His legs and arms. They have all been produced in their circular shape, flat on the back, rounded in front, cabochon-style according to jewellers, either by machinery or by intense and long-term physical labour. I personally prefer to think the crucifix as a whole was made by the passionate fidelity and patience of a Christian long long ago, and I have resisted offers to submit the metal and the workmanship to the dating techniques of modern science. Truth is all very well, but there is a difference between scientific truth – the exposure of fakes and fraud – and the truths superimposed on inanimate objects by love and by faith.

'Values also differ. The crucifix is obviously worth a considerable sum of money in the estimation of auctioneers and mercenary folk, but I consider it priceless, more valuable than any valuation. Unfortunately, last January, somebody who was feeling greedy, and ready to break the laws of the land and the rules of decency took advantage of my policy of leaving our church unlocked. He shut his mind to the value of the crucifix for people like me, pocketed it, and stole the money in the box for contributions to the upkeep of the building.

'No judgment, please, of the somebody involved, not yet – wait for the story to unfold.

'To the best of my knowledge, gleaned in recent days, the crucifix has changed hands several times in the months of its truancy, and, more importantly than the terms of its transfer from one owner to the next, more worthy of record in a sermon in a house of God, left a trail of strange occurrences in its wake. Thus, the somebody with the crucifix in his pocket realised that it would be difficult to sell without risk, disposed of it, threw it away, and in the act of doing so almost killed himself in a motorbike accident. Part-time owner number two believes she miscarried and lost her child because she was given the crucifix and cashed it in. A learned gentleman with terminal cancer bought it in order to argue that it was neither Christian nor holy, to advance atheistic views, to advance negative views, but died of concluding that he had been wrong. Another gentleman is under the impression that it tempted him and punished him for yielding to temptation. The same applies to the lady who gave us back our crucifix – she wishes to remain anonymous, but we must all remember her in our prayers. No doubt, other innocent and guilty receivers of our property experienced the phenomenon of unaccountable benefits of ownership, leading to mistakes, more or less sharp corrective action, and a strong drive to pass the crucifix on to someone else.

'The implications are hard to credit. They suggest that the crucifix has the power to mete out even life or death. They suggest it's a potential friend or enemy, a moralist, a court of law, and a type of boomerang, a thinking boomerang, planning and plotting its journey back to base.

'I have another piece of evidence to bring to your notice. Not only the crucifix has been returned to us, but also every single penny that was stolen.

'My aim today was to lay these facts before you dispassionately. But I feel I must speak for myself to the extent of rejoicing, as the birthday of our Lord approaches, the day we all celebrate at Christmas, that my ministry has already received wonderful gifts, the gifts of hope fulfilled and faith confirmed.

'The crucifix has therefore, perhaps, been

responsible for those happy returns or beneficial effects. Yet I would not pretend or presume to be bearing witness to a miracle. Every one of the examples I have quoted is attributable to self-hypnosis, human error or coincidence. I readily admit that the crucifix, since its installation here in 1872, has shown no sign whatsoever of being anything more than pieces of metal and semi-precious stones. Nevertheless, I cannot deny that the adjective miraculous may be applied to the latest chapter of its story, although I would rather describe the sequence of events as another of the mysteries of religion, which we have to choose either to reject or accept.

'Religion in our poor old country has been going through a bad patch. Frivolity and escapism, politics and idolatry, and especially science and technology, have replaced it to a certain extent. But science cannot explain the universe – how it began, where it is – better or more logically than the Book of Genesis, and technology is cold comfort in our latter days. In modern terms, God is one of the innumerable "free offers" we are assailed by. Belief in God remains a matter of choice. You are at liberty to choose whether or not you are willing to bow your heads and bend your knees and acknowledge that there are things you don't know, that we don't know, and more than likely never will. Forgive me for warning you that in a crisis, when the earth moves against you, when the almost inevitable strikes you or me personally, it's much easier to swallow a mystery than to pray to a machine. I choose to see the hand of God in all the expressions of nature and life, however mysterious His ways, His justice, and even in the vicissitudes of our crucifix.

'A few words more and I shall have done: they are that I can't quite decide whether or not to lock the door of the church in future.

'Thank you for your attention. The hymn we are going to sing is not only a comfort to a man of my calling at my time of life. Today the world is full of dangers and fearfulness: in other words, it is the same as ever. For everyone, for everyone who cares for anyone or anything, for the sake of all of you and for God's sake, let's sing hymn number twenty-seven in your hymn-books, *Abide with me.*'

The Publishers hope that this book has given you enjoyable reading. Large Print Books are especially designed to be as easy to see and hold as possible. If you wish a complete list of our books please ask at your local library or write directly to:

Ulverscroft Large Print Books
Anstey, Leicester, England.
Thorpe, North America.

This Large Print Book, for people
who cannot read normal print,
is published under the auspices of

THE ULVERSCROFT FOUNDATION

... we hope you have enjoyed this book.
Please think for a moment about those
who have worse eyesight than you ...
and are unable to even read or enjoy
Large Print without great difficulty.

You can help them by sending a
donation, large or small, to:

**The Ulverscroft Foundation,
1, The Green, Bradgate Road,
Anstey, Leicestershire, LE7 7FU,
England.**
or request a copy of our brochure for
more details.

The Foundation will use all donations
to assist those people who are visually
impaired and need special attention
with medical research, diagnosis
and treatment.

Thank you very much for your help.